SEMPER DIE

by

Jonathan Shuerger

Prologue

It is a truth universally acknowledged that in the nightmare of the zombie apocalypse, the pizza boxes die first.

Oh, come on, that was a good line. Cut me some slack, it's my first time writing a book, and Jane Austen is one of the few books that can be reliably gotten. Took me forever to come up with it.

Guess I should probably tell you what a 'pizza box' is, huh? You can probably tell, I'm new with the writing thing.

A pizza box is the lowest qualification rank on the rifle range; the emblem is a square with a bullseye set on it. The few, proud and brave call it a pizza box.

And pizza boxes dying is not an operational doctrine; it's a cold fact. Every shot counts now. We have *thousands* of cannibal freaks roaming around, swarming to rip and feast on anything living they can reach. The chaff is getting sorted from the wheat real quick, and the low scorers with their accompanying excuses are dying out like lightning bugs in an air fryer.

The Marine Corps never had the most numbers. We like that expeditionary lifestyle; light, fast and set to blast. But since July 4, 2016, we're an even smaller and leaner Corps. The fat's been cut. The malingerers and waivers we had are dead by now, torn up by brother Z or shot for dereliction under the new UCMJ.

Only ones left now are the killers, and that's how we like it.

So, to all that hear these presents, greetings. My name is Sergeant Alexander Slaughter, 0331 machine gunner in God's majestic Marine Corps.

Yeah, yeah, I know. Ah'll Slaughter. The instructors at SOI heard my name and immediately made me hump the M240; they thought it was funny.

This is the record of Alpha Squad, Bravo Company, 2nd

Battalion, 2nd Marines, 2nd Marine Division. We're being 'incentivized' to write these; apparently the few nerds that survived the Collapse want to compile a history of the day overpopulation stopped being a problem. Ordinarily, I'd say screw'em and do something useful with my time, but they're paying me an extra hundred dollars every two weeks for it.

I've done worse for less, to be honest, so here we are.

Before I dive into it, a couple of things.

This record will be true. I may not paint every Marine in it as a hero, but none of them died as cowards, and I'm not lying about any of them. My integrity means something, and I'm not selling my honor so nerds like you read this.

And the other thing... Gunny Hudson didn't allow profanity in the squad. Therefore, it will not be present here. That man may be gone, but I ain't seen his body and there's a track record now of the dead getting back up.

Chapter 1 - EXERCISE

MONDAY
JULY 4, 2016
1337 ZULU

"Comm check."

Something banged in the back of the Humvee. Sounded expensive.

"They're not answering."

"That's not what I frigging asked for, was it, Marine? Comm check."

"Whatever, man. Whiskey Oscar Quebec, Whiskey Oscar Quebec, this is Lima Charlie Delta. How do you read, over?"

Next to me, Gunnery Sergeant James Hudson wiped his forehead with his cammy sleeve and heaved his weight onto the reluctant battery. We already had the passenger seat taken out of the truck to get at them, but something had warped the housing on this particular Humvee and it was a battle to wrench the dead unit out. You'd think Motor T could hit it with some pliers, but then again, it was a miracle any of our Gulf-One-era vics were operational. I chose not to question and/or anger the dark sorcerers who kept our thirty-year-old junk from falling apart.

Gunny's face screwed up in effort as he pushed on that battery, and I reached over to shove on it myself one-handed.

"Come on, you stupid son of a—"

"Language, Sergeant," Gunny warned, his voice strained.

"Aye, Gunny," I responded, trying not to roll my eyes. *We're in the United States Marine Corps, Gunny. Profanity is professional.*

Gunny's eyes narrowed for a second, then he punched the battery. With a *chunk*, the battery slipped into the housing. "There we go," Gunny said with a grin and a groan. "You can pound on that all you want, but self-control with the right touch will win every time."

I had to smile back. "Aye, Gunny," I said. "You write fortune cookies, too?"

"No one asked you, Sergeant," he said. "Go check your Marines; I'll get the seat back in."

I chuckled and said, "Oorah, Gunny."

I headed to the back of the Humvee, where Alpha Squad's comm specialist Lance Corporal Dakota hunkered over the radio, headset over his ears. The device was unspeakably ancient. Paul Revere had probably warned Concord and Lexington with this exact PRC-117. The thing was basically gasping dust from its housing, but our S-6 necromancers refused to let it die as long as it could be useful.

I shook my head, wondering at how everything could go so wrong.

One more thing....

This exercise had gone FUBAR in pretty much every way possible. We were on loan from Camp Lejeune to the Basic School, helping birth some brand new baby officers into the world just before July 4 weekend hit. Well, the LTs were morons, big surprise, and one of the vics they 'checked' for us had a bad battery unit. Friday, the day we were supposed to End-Ex, 1st Fireteam's Humvee refused to start. We tried to jump it. No good. It was dead dead, not the kind that could come back, ironically enough.

This started a cascade of wondrous military efficiency.

We called back for a new battery, but the corporal on range control was too busy swapping sex stories with his buddies to pass the info on. By the time that ASVAB waiver remembered to pass on the request, Motor T had released early for the weekend, leaving one poor private—lowest on the totem pole, no doubt—to check us in whenever we got back. Unfortunately, no one gave the kid the keys to the equipment cage and his sergeant had turned off his phone, no doubt getting wasted already.

We therefore camped in the middle of the range for two

frigging days, waiting for someone to show up and give us a battery. Leaving the vic on the range wasn't an option; if the local Sergeant Major, aka sadge madge, caught wind of us abandoning gear in the field, he'd rip the elasticity out of our virgin rectums.

So, we stayed.

Naturally, the LTs were already on their 'well-deserved' liberty, leaving us dumb schmucks to make our MREs stretch a couple extra days while we camped in the middle of a TBS range.

Thank God for Gunny Hudson.

I'd wind up saying that a lot in the next couple days. Gunny was an instructor for a different class of LTs than the one we were supporting, but once he caught wind of our situation, that man dropped his BBQ tongs and powered back to base. Somehow, he conjured some keys for the battery cage—or more likely, broke the lock, knowing what I know now—grabbed a couple batteries, and drove his personal SUV onto the range to hand-deliver the gear.

You can't find staff NCOs like that anymore, and every Marine in the squad felt a surge of immediate loyalty and protectiveness. Offers of free chow and/or sex acts showered onto Hudson like rice at a wedding.

Of course, he acted like he didn't care. "Anything for my Marines," he said, and that was that.

I miss him.

Anyway, just to add onto the deluxe crapcake stack, now Range Control wasn't responding with our permission to exit the range, and Lance Corporal Dakota was starting to look a little upset.

"How's it coming?" I asked.

Dakota slumped and held up the headset. "I don't know, Sergeant. Twelve hundred, I got a response. Thirteen hundred, no response. I've been checking every five minutes since."

Corporal Sloane leaned against the back of the Humvee, his thumbs hooked in his vest as he rhythmically banged his kevlar against the metal of the vic. "I think his azimuth's wrong."

"Wasn't wrong an hour ago, corporal," Dakota shot back. "And we haven't moved. Whatever it is, is on their end."

Sloane shrugged and glanced at me. "You get the battery in there, Sergeant?"

I grinned at him. "Always do. Tight fit, just like always, but nothing some tender love and lube can't help."

Sloane smiled, his dark eyes tired. He'd pulled two hour-long watches last night, spaced out three hours apart, and his Monsters had run out a couple days ago. From the wad in his lip, he was sucking on some MRE coffee grounds to stay awake.

"I thought I heard violence, Sergeant?"

"Yeah, that's how Gunny's generation showed love. Go over there; he says he loves you, too."

Sloane shook his head. "Nope, I'm good."

"That's what I thought. Get us packed up. We're hitting the road."

"Heard," he said, with a sigh of relief. He pushed off the truck and shouted, "Alpha, load up!"

Groans and curses met his words as Alpha Squad lurched to their feet. Packs lifted off the ground and landed in the back of the Humvees, while corporals Sloane, Garrett and Martinez paced around, taking accountability of weapons and serialized gear. Four Marines piled into each of the three Humvees. Our Navy corpsman, Doc Ramon, elected to ride with 2nd.

The mutters were heartfelt.

"Finally."

"Thank God."

"Hey, you think Gunny needs a girlfriend?"

"I don't think he's into used gear, Sanchez."

"Shut up, Ferreira!"

As I walked past 2nd Fireteam's vic, Lance Corporal Ferreira stuck his head out the window and shouted, "Hey, Sergeant! When we get our phones back?"

I answered. "Soon as we get back, Furry."

He grinned, doing this stupid head-bob that made him look like a grade-A retard. "Oorah, Sergeant."

I continued, not missing a beat. "And after we clean weapons, turn 'em in, clean the Humvees, turn 'em in and hold a safety brief."

The smile dropped off his face. "Man. Why you gotta do that to me? My girl's waiting on me."

"Because I feed off of sadness and fear, Lance Corporal, and because your right hand will always forgive you for making it wait. Now stick your grape back in your cage and lock it up."

With a grumbled "Aye, Sergeant," he complied.

I rounded the Humvee to see Gunny Hudson leaning on the Humvee. The seat was already back in and the dead batteries stowed in his vic. "Good to go?" he asked amiably.

"Yes, Gunny. Again, can't thank you enough for this."

A stern look came over his grizzled face. "Shouldn't have happened in the first place. I'll have a talk with Hauptmann about his class leaving you high and dry like this. They're going to learn how to be leaders of Marines, I promise."

I grimaced. I almost felt bad for those baby LTs.

But not really.

Behind us, engines growled as the HMMWVs started up, every last one of them idling roughly.

He slapped the hood of the Humvee, shouting to be heard over the engine roar. "That's our cue. Let's get you back and get you some hot chow. Ride with me."

"You got it, Gunny."

We synced up comms, performed basic vehicle checks and pulled out.

****

It took about forty-five minutes to hit the gate from the range. We trucked along old roads, the sunlight gleaming through the leaves of the trees with noonday rays. It was July, but it wasn't freaking hot yet. Not like Twenty-Nine Palms or Yuma.

Course, it wasn't *Pendleton* and its sandy beaches, either. That would have been sweet, but God didn't love me that much.

The first inkling we had of the FUBAR situation to come was an abandoned truck on the side of the road, pointing the other way. It wasn't a HMMWV. It was a civvy white Ford F-150, one of the three models of vehicles Marines bought themselves with their boot camp pay. It was pretty, too.

Gunny grunted. "Must be an NCO model, huh?"

I grinned. With shiny rims like that? Yeah.

Something kinda itched at me about it, and I turned back to look as we passed. I didn't see anybody around it.

"Gunny?"

"Yeah, Sergeant?"

I hiked a thumb that way. "Why are they heading down-range?"

Gunny opened his mouth, then closed it. It was July 4 liberty. There was no reason to go onto an active training range unless they were bailing idiots like us out.

His steely green eyes flicked in the rearview mirror to watch the truck receding in the distance. "And why is a pretty truck like that abandoned?"

After a minute of silence, he growled, "Call it in. Let Law Enforcement take care of it."

I nodded and pulled out my cell.

He and I were old GWOT, Global War On Terror, with several Afghanistan and Iraq deployments between us. Abandoned vics were pretty much always VBIEDs, or vehicle-born improvised explosive devices. We might be stateside, but we'd lost too many friends in places they were supposed to be safe.

Law Enforcement Battalion was probably bored out of their minds right now anyway, since all the lance criminals were off-base, wrecking civilian jurisdiction. I found LE in my contacts, mashed the screen and settled into my seat.

Ring.

Ring.

Ring.

Nothing. I glared at the screen.

Ring.

Ring.

Ring.

Gunny glanced at me. "They haven't picked up yet? What else do they have to do?"

I checked my phone. Plenty of bars, no lost connection. They just weren't picking it up.

"That makes *two*—," I said slowly, "—Marine units not responding to call-ins. Range and now LE."

"Yes," Gunny said. "Yes, it does."

We drove on. I could hear the wheels turning in Gunny's head as the convoy proceeded.

We hit nice roads, which meant Quantico proper. We were about five minutes out from Motor T at this point.

"Try Fire," Gunny said, his voice grim. I was already searching it in my contacts list.

Ring.

Ring.

Ring.

Same thing. No pick up.

My radio crackled. "Sierra Sierra, this is Lima Charlie Golf. How read, over?"

Gutierrez. I gripped the radio set on my vest and pressed the button. "Lima Charlie Golf, this is Sierra Sierra. What's up, over?"

"Boss, is that smoke north? Uh, over?"

I twisted to look that way. Sure enough, a black pillar climbed into the sky, marring the beautiful sunshine with a column of ink.

Without warning, Gunny wrenched the wheel over and

braked hard. The SUV skidded through some dirt and threw some rocks to the side of the road.

I let out a yelped curse, but Gunny was so distracted, he didn't even call me on it. His eyes were riveted in front of him. Behind us, the convoy fell in.

The focus in his eyes jolted me. I turned to see what he saw.

It was the gate. It was empty, and it was wide open.

The gate to *Quantico*. America's brass throne, the country club of military mingling, where generals and CEOs contracted multi-billion-dollar weapons deals for the next round of freedom we lower schlubs were going to deliver.

Both of us stared at this impossible, improbable, possibly illegal sight. There should have been minimum four unlucky Marines from LE or fap units standing there, holding M4s, pistols on their hips, hating their lives and checking IDs while officer spouses demanded they call them by their husbands' ranks.

Instead, trash blew across the street, flying into empty guard huts with doors ajar.

"Sergeant."

"Yeah, Gunny?"

"You got angels?"

I nodded grimly. "Yes, Gunny, we do."

"Get 'em up here."

****

Every time Marines go out on exercise, we take our weapons. For us infantry, that meant M4s; unlucky POGs still carried the longer M16s, but who really cares. The rifles would be Condition Four while in CONUS, which means that we'd have mags in, but no rounds. No one wanted devils unaliving themselves or others on exercise. It still wouldn't matter when we got back; armory would make us clean the rifles anyway so they wouldn't have to do it.

But still, since we were carrying several hundred thousand dollars of military-issued equipment, we assigned one Marine in every vic to Guardian Angel status. These Marines carried live rounds in the extremely unlikely scenario someone tried to hijack a Marine convoy, which still makes me chuckle with evil joy when I think about it.

Three vics meant three Marines with two mags per. Each mag contained thirty rounds of 5.56. One hundred and eighty rounds fired by pissed-off-but-suddenly-excited Marines would ruin most carjackers' day.

I liked for my fireteam leaders to assign their own angels and just inform me who it was. It was a chance to give a new kid some responsibility, sober them up while on exercise. Of course, I'd vet those choices. I'm not riding with a dude whose mental was teetering on the Cliff of Insanity.

This time, I had PFC Marshal, LCPL Dominguez and LCPL Turner. I signaled the other Marines to hang back with the trucks; no reason to put Marines into live firing lanes holding empty rifles.

Gunny stepped around his SUV, checking the chamber of a Glock 19 and racking the slide.

I glanced at him. "That's illegal on base, Gunny."

He gave me a wry look. "So, call LE."

I conceded that with a rueful nod. The man had a way of making a point.

"Stays in the glove compartment, most of the time. But…," and he slid the weapon into the back of his jeans, "just in case three separate Marine units *aren't* all jacking off at the same time while the gate is unmanned, I'll keep it here."

I moved forward, taking Turner's extra mag and slotting it in. "All right, Marines, huddle up. We're Condition One, but *do not fire* without my okay, good to go?"

"Aye, Sergeant," they chorused quietly. Clicks and snaps sounded as mags slammed home in the wells. Their eyes kept moving around, continuously scanning the area as they loaded. Good for them. They weren't stupid.

"I'm not kidding," I said. "The last thing I need is to do paperwork on one of you idiots because you shot a general's wife on frigging Quantico. Keep your finger straight and off the trigger, hear me?"

Nods and "Aye, Sergeant."

"Out of curiosity, Sergeant, under what circumstances *would* we open fire?" Dominguez asked.

Gunny joined the huddle. "Under one condition only, devil. If your life or the lives of your fellow Marines are in danger," he said, "you kill, and you kill fast."

That sobered him.

"Aye, Gunny."

He glanced at me. "Take 'em in, Sergeant."

I nodded, feeling my muscles tighten with pre-combat tension. "Oorah, Gunny. On me, Marines."

Rifles to shoulders, eyeballs to ACOGs and sphincters clenched, the Marines of Alpha moved into Quantico.

Chapter 2 – MONSTERS

Smoothly and quietly, my ad hoc fireteam moved through the gate. Turner and Marshal swept the approaches, their rifles moving in tandem with their sightline, their cheeks pressed to the stocks of their rifles. Whenever a weapon passed across a Marine, the muzzle dropped to the ground, then came right back up.

Because we're professionals, and professionals don't wanna get shot if they don't have to be.

Marine Corps bases have a feel to them; everyone says so. Going onto a Marine Corps base, you can sense the anger, the harshness of our culture.

I can't tell you how many times I've heard an airman ask why we're all so mad all time. That's just our faces, man. And also, the Corps sucks.

When we showed up a week ago, in our green service alphas and TDY orders fresh in hand, Quantico felt like an HOA run by Marine Corps brass. Officers everywhere, uniforms pristine, cars with the rank stickers on the windshields; it was a whole different world. The lawns were manicured, the sidewalks swept, the MPs straight-backed and perfect. It felt tight, tense, as if every eye judged you and waited for you to mess up so you could get punished.

It kinda still felt like that now, but for a whole different reason.

A grocery bag from the MCX drifted across the road before us. A puff of wind caught it and tossed it into the air, where it lazily turned as it sank back down to the asphalt.

We stared at it.

It was trash.

On Quantico.

The most uptight station in the Marine Corps.

Back then, I was pretty sure the death penalty was still active for that kind of negligence.

"I got a bad feeling about this, boss," Dominguez muttered. He was a good kid; still green, no deployments under his belt yet. Eager, teachable, and some kind of vow against alcohol, which prevented most stupidity Marine 03s can get into.

I know NCOs aren't supposed to have favorites, so he's definitely not mine.

I glanced at him. "You and me both, Dom. Head on a swivel," I said.

"Aye, Sergeant."

We scooted across the street, knees bent, rifles covering every angle. Nothing living moved. But we saw some weird stuff.

Doors broken in. Shattered windows. A car overturned on the lawn. Smoke rising in the distance.

"Sergeant?" Marshal asked, his voice confused.

I glanced over at him, saw him looking down. I shifted to join him, and soon joined his confusion, too.

Splashes of rust-colored brown on the sidewalk. Footprints and handprints both. Now that we were looking, we could see the same color on the green grass considered so sacred by sergeants major everywhere.

"What the h—?" Marshal started to say.

"Belay that," Gunny said. We glanced at him, surprised at the order, but his face was hard. "Keep control of yourselves, keep an eye out. Whatever's going on, losing our heads isn't going to help."

My guys glanced at me, and I nodded. "Gunny's right. Let's go."

Something popped in the distance, very distinct, but I still didn't believe my ears. A few seconds later, again.

"That's an M9," Turner said.

"Staff NCO or officer," I said. "Maybe they know what's going on."

"Blood and gunfire on Quantico," Dominguez muttered. "This can't go wrong."

We moved as a unit away from the blood, keeping our spacing tight. Gunny's sidearm was out now, and I didn't blame him. Whatever was going on was weird enough that getting in trouble for a sidearm wasn't likely to rank real high on our concerns.

I clicked the radio at my collarbone. "Martinez."

A second later, 1st Fireteam Leader's voice came over. "Dad? You're not using callsigns. How'm I supposed to believe it's you if—?"

"Shut up; we're not playing Marines anymore," I said. "We got blood on the ground, debris and some gunfire in the distance. We're moving to assist whoever it is. Get the squad into the gatehouse and scavenge their extra ammo, if any. Break open the safe if you have to. Advise when you're done."

"Oorah, Sergeant. Heading out."

We moved.

****

Quantico did not improve the further in we moved. There was trash everywhere on the streets, spilled garbage cans, blowing paper and wrappers. We saw streaks of browning blood on the sidewalks, a few hours old. An abandoned LE vehicle sat nearby, door open.

"This is why LE isn't answering," Gunny muttered. We checked the car. No weapon, no ammo. Whoever drove this had already stripped it.

More pops. Closer together this time. Something screamed in the distance.

"That… didn't sound human," Marshal said, pointing a finger in the general direction.

"If it bleeds, we can kill it," Turner muttered.

"Lock it up," I said, before we got any jumpier than we already were. "Let's go."

We covered the distance rapidly, bounding by twos. More gunfire sounded in the distance now, not just the pistol we were closing in on.

The weapon fired again. Sounded close now.

"It's on this block," Gunny said.

We were surrounded by command element buildings. Windows had been shattered on several floors of the structures. Cars and trucks had slammed into one another, three of them turned over and still burning.

The pistol fired again, close. Something howled in the distance, the sound weird and distorted by the echo.

"That one," I said, pointing at a Division HQ. "Move in."

Marshal and Dominguez bounded up, each taking a corner of the entry way. The glass doors had been broken; I saw loose brass on the concrete. Turner, Gunny and I surged through the door, stomping through the broken glass and kicking bullet casings across the floor. I shouted, "United States Marines!"

And that's when we saw our first one.

A man twisted around at the end of the darkened command hallway. Fluorescent lights flickered, flashing across him and turning him into some kind of horror character. It was impossible to make out any detail on his face, but he arched very strangely, craning his neck. He tilted his head, as if listening to us rather than looking at us.

He hunched over instead of standing straight, holding his hands out like claws in front of him. I could make out the jeans and polo shirt he was wearing. Splashes of something dark discolored the garments.

Bodies lay on the floor around him, unmoving silhouettes, at least eight of them. He had been hunched over one before we burst in.

"Boss…," Turner started, then the man started to charge.

****

To be clear, this was not an ordinary run.

I'd seen people respond to armed Marines barging into their civilian spaces. There is always fear, a shrinking back from the sheer volume we emit. I've seen rooms drop to the ground, people covering their heads, even crying.

I had never once seen a man drop his head and barrel toward me on a straight line, arms pumping wildly, howling like asthmatic Satan.

I made the call.

My M4 barked twice before I could even think twice. The man jerked from center mass impacts and tumbled to the side, clawing at the wall beside him. The timbre of that weird yowl changed. I'd hit him in the lungs.

My barrel dipped out of habit.

"Sergeant!" Gunny yelled.

I thought he was trying to chew me out for putting the guy down, so I twisted back to him to explain, but he wasn't even looking at me.

Gunny Hudson marched forward, his Glock bucking in his hand and snapping shots off. I whipped back around and saw the thing struggling back to its feet.

"Oh, you are kidding me," I said, and unloaded on him, jerking on the trigger non-stop. The dude blasted backwards as rounds tore through his chest. I must have shot him eight times in two seconds.

I moved up on him and aimed my weapon right at his forehead. This frakker was still moving, his arms and legs writhing on the floor. I pulled the trigger, slopping the contents of the man's skull out the back of his head.

He finally stopped moving.

Turner, Marshal and Dominguez stood behind me, their jaws on the floor.

"What was *that*, Sergeant?" Marshal asked.

I shook my head, still shaken by shooting a fellow American. "I don't know. Adrenaline? Drugs, maybe? That can keep a guy up for a bit."

Gunny squatted down next to the corpse. "He's not bleeding," he said quietly.

I looked at him. "That's impossible. I shot him like twenty

times."

Gunny nodded. "Yeah, I see the holes. They aren't bleeding, though."

"Uh," Dominguez stammered, "what does that mean, Gunny?"

"It means," I said as Gunny lifted himself back to his feet, "that this guy was already dead when we shot him."

****

They stared at me. "What do you mean," Marshal said, "he was *already dead?*"

Something howled upstairs, and in the stairwell next to us, we heard footsteps pounding down the stairs. Something slammed into the pushbar doors, scratching at the metal.

Then something else hit. And something else. A lot of somethings, all screaming.

As one, we made the decision to back away, rifles raised, just as the door sprang open and a wave of people spilled out.

I'm using the term "people" very loosely, because we could suddenly see these ones just fine.

Their eyes were wide stares, devoid of pupils or irises, just sick red orbs glowing in the dark. Their skin had paled to translucence, which made a really nice background for all the blood crusting their mouths and fingers. Scarlet liquid fanned down the fronts of their chests, and they lurched towards us, snarling with bestial fury.

"Marines, drop 'em!" I roared, and the muzzle flashes of four M4s lit up the room.

Gobbets of wet flesh blew from the backs of our attackers, spattering against the wall and the faces of those in the back. The impacts rocked the crowd backwards, but none of them fell over.

"They're not dying, Sergeant!" Turner yelled.

"Keep it up!" I shouted back. The barrage of gunfire was intense; I was already mostly deaf. We formed a line of rifles, spitting lines of fire into the drugged-out horde. A second later, my bolt rammed back and my trigger clicked.

Empty.

Made sense. I'd dumped most of my mag into the first guy.

I reached back, gripped Marshal's extra mag and ejected my empty. I slammed the second one in, tapped the bottom just in case it didn't lock, slapped the bolt home and sighted back in.

Empty to full, 2.5 seconds.

I was about to open back up when I heard the distinctive crack of M9 fire. The pistol barked behind us, and one of the attackers threw her hands up and toppled backwards, a hole in her forehead. Another crack, and a red-eyed Marine in cammies crumpled face first on the deck, his skull blasted out.

"Headshots!" a gravelly voice roared, and involuntarily, we adjusted our aimpoints accordingly.

At the range of eight yards, we popped their grapes like wet blisters, splattering gore across the white cinderblock walls. This had far more effect than center mass shots. Bodies hit the deck, sprawling and tangling those behind. When we were done, the bodies of twenty people, all that weird sickly pale color, tumbled across the floor of the command hallway.

We turned to see who our new ally was, and my heart sank.

Three chevrons up, four down, star in the center; that's how the ditty went. My drill instructors had screamed it at me and made me scream it back for thirteen weeks on the Island. Marines learned by the ditty, and you screamed the ditty.

I was fourteen years out of Parris Island. I did not scream the ditty this time, though I did very much want to scream. **Instead, I said, "Good afternoon, Sergeant Major."**

Chapter 3 – CONDITION ONE

"Welcome to the show, Marines."

That was how he greeted us. He had sergeant major rank on his cammies, which he was wearing despite the fact he should have been on July 4 libo. His name tape read HAWKE.

Sgt Major Hawke was a massive black Marine with muscled arms exploding out of sleeves rolled so sharp, they could cut a hajji in half. There was nothing behind his eyes, nothing but the endless void of God's Marine Corps.

We'd all seen it. First sergeants and sergeants major all had it. They'd been in so long the Corps had ejected their souls like a spent mag and replaced it with the Marine Corps Handbook. They lived to eat the lower enlisted alive and make second lieutenants piss themselves.

All three of my lower enlisted stood straighter immediately.

Hawke looked at them. "Good afternoon, Marines," he said in a voice way too deep to be human.

"Good afternoon, Sergeant Major," they responded.

He stepped closer to Marshal, his eyes locked on the kid's chin.

Ah, crap, I thought.

"How old is that shave, devil?" he rumbled.

He had some scrabble, for sure. Marshal looked like he wanted to join the bodies on the floor right then. "Uh, couple days, Sergeant Major?"

"Couple days," Hawke repeated, his voice toneless. "And that's acceptable to you, Marine?"

I stepped forward, my butthole clenching at the treatment to come. I mean, he was going to light into me as his squad leader *anyway*....

"Got stuck out on exercise before liberty kicked off, Sergeant Major. It's not his fault; it was my call to reserve the water for drinking."

Sgt Major looked over at me, his eyes chewing me up and spitting me out, learning everything about me. "That so, Gunny?"

Hudson nodded. "Yes, Sergeant Major. Bad battery in the HMMWV. I just delivered them a replacement and brought them in."

"Hmm."

Hawke turned back to Marshal. "You got your razor?"

Marshal nodded. Thank God he did.

Hawke pointed. "Get in the bathroom now and shave. You don't got water, piss on the blade. It's not the end of the world *yet*."

Marshal glanced at me. "Uh, aye, Sergeant Major."

"Check the stalls first," Hawke rumbled, and turned away. "They like to hide."

"Turner," I said, trying not to roll my eyes at the lack of priorities here. "Battle buddy. Go."

Turner snapped a quick nod, then moved with Marshal to the male head down the hallway. They kicked in the door, checked it, then disappeared inside. A second later, I heard stall doors kicked open.

Sgt Major turned back to me and Gunny. "So why are you here, Sergeant?"

I pointed at his sidearm. "We saw the gate was down, LE and Fire didn't respond, heard your shots. We came to check it out."

"You and every possessed maniac on the base," Hawke growled. "You put so much gunfire out, every one of those freaks will be here soon. I was rationing my shots, good to go? They don't respond to single shots, not like they do to mag-dumping kids like you."

"Yeah, you're welcome, Sergeant Major," I bit off, just before Gunny Hudson slid between us.

"Thank you, Sergeant," he said quietly. "I'm sure the Sergeant Major is grateful for the assist."

Before Hawke could unload on him, Gunny asked, "Do

you have armory access, Sergeant Major? We got a full squad of Marines at the gate that need rounds. All we have are Sergeant Slaughter's guardian angels and they're running low."

Hawke nodded slowly, his eyes still burning into me. "Roger that, Gunny. Sergeant, radio your Marines and have them meet us here."

He pointed at a map of the base, at an intersection a quarter mile away. "And Sergeant?"

"Yes, Sergeant Major?"

Hawke's eyes pierced mine with age-old hate. "Make sure they got shaves."

****

"Hold up, he said *what?*"

I closed my eyes and repeated, "Make sure the guys have fresh shaves."

The radio squawked, "Yeah, I heard *what* you said, Sergeant. Is he out of his mind?"

I sighed. "He's old Corps. Been too long in garrison. What do you want me to say, Martinez? Do it. Make sure it's done."

"Aye, Sergeant. Be there soon. Gonna have to share razors, though."

"I think infection is the least of your worries right now," I said drily.

Once Turner and Marshal got out of the head, faces freshly shaved and bleeding, we headed out down the street. Dominguez got off easy, but his baby face never needed shaving anyway. I, having experience with garrison Marine Corps, shaved every day in the field, just in case I got called into a meeting with a bunch of snot-nosed lieutenants looking for something to pick on.

We didn't see any more of the crazed people-that-didn't-bleed on our way over. Most of the base was abandoned, since everybody was on July 4 liberty. Knowing what I know now, that fact probably saved our lives.

We reached the armory just as the rest of Alpha pulled in with the Humvees. Sgt Major pulled out an access card and swiped us in through the chainlink gate, then the armory itself.

No Marines inside; again, it was July 4.

I started giving orders. "We need 5.56 and frags. Throw a few cans on the tables so we can load mags, put the rest in the vics. Sanchez, Furry, grab boxes for your SAWs, if you can find them. Grenades go to Martinez; he'll dish them out. Turnboe, Stevens, you're on fire watch. You see any movement, *anything*, you call it out."

The squad stepped to fast, without the bellyaching that normally accompanied having to do anything associated with work. Having a sadge madge around was a help, sometimes.

The Marines had the trucks loaded in five minutes, then gathered around the weapons cleaning tables to load their weapons. Each Marine took six mags and started pushing rounds down into them. I could hear the disquieted mutter as Turner, Marshal and Dominguez shared the firefight in the HQ with them.

I joined Gunny and Hawke at their table and started loading my own mags. Both of them were already on their fourth. The M4 looked like a freaking toy across Sgt Major's huge chest.

He had his phone out and had just tapped on a newsfeed. The volume was low enough that only we could hear it.

"*...outbreak is everywhere, Janet! What isn't the government telling us?*"

"*All I'm saying is we should remain calm and see—*"

"*Hold on. Folks, we have a situation downstairs and they're telling us to evacuate. A crowd is… is forcing its way through the doors.*"

Screams sounded in the background, with the sound of shattering glass and that same weird howl we'd already heard. "*They're in the studio! Cut the feed! Cut the f—!*"

The phone went blank.

"What," Gunny breathed, "is going on?"

Sgt Major looked grim. "That was Richmond. My Twitter feed is full of the same. Something's hit us, hit us hard, and people are turning into animals. I've seen videos of civilians eating people in the middle of the street. And it's not just the U.S. It's all over the place."

I looked from him to Gunny. "So, what is it?"

Sgt Major shrugged. "Bioweapon, probably airborne. Al-Qaeda, China, or some corporate idiots. Doesn't matter."

He looked from me to Gunny, his eyes blazing against his black skin. "Nothing's changed for us. We are Marines. We will confront this new threat and we will emerge victorious."

He pulled up a maps app on his phone and showed us. "Last I heard from higher, a fallback point was established an hour west of here, at Belfair Crossroads. It's in the country, lower population, fewer affected individuals."

Hawke looked at me. "That's probably what spared your squad, Sergeant; being in the field."

I felt my breathing go shallow involuntarily, and I took a deep breath to combat the anxiety. "Do you think it's still in the air?"

Gunny spread his hands. "We're all okay. Most airborne pathogens deteriorate fast. If it is still spreading, it's not in the air anymore."

Sgt Major shrugged. "Or we're resistant."

I glanced at him. "When did it start? Do you know?"

"Heard the first reports this morning," he growled, "listening to my podcast on my drive in at oh five hundred. Didn't pay much attention; it was all just idiot libs in the cities protesting Independence Day. Blocking streets, holding up traffic, climate change crap. Then more reports came out, and they all started sounded the same. Civilians biting civilians, unconfirmed reports of red eyes. By the time I flipped the news on, they said most of the camera crews in the affected areas were not responding."

I twirled my finger in the air, indicating all of Quantico.

"And here? Any kind of recall issued?"

Hawke grunted. "All the Marines are on libo, probably partying in Virginia Beach and drunk out of their minds."

I nodded. "Phones are off."

Gunny chuckled darkly. "If they have any sense."

"Boss?"

It was Martinez. He had one hand on his rig, the other on his rifle, and peered outside the fence. The Marines were with him, their voices falling to whispers. "You might wanna look at this."

I pushed away from the table and jogged over to him. The disquiet from our conversation was creeping up on me now, and I felt my body juicing with adrenaline. I was getting combat ready.

"What's up, Martinez?"

He pointed. "Check it out."

I glanced where he showed me, back where we had collected the sergeant major from.

Smoke from the distant fires blew across the base, reducing visibility to about three hundred yards. But I saw what he did.

Figures stumbled through the smoke, walking slow and stiff.

"Those survivors?" LCPL Turner asked.

I raised my M4 and zeroed in on the closest one through the optic.

It was a woman, typical officer wife type. Hot, great body, lots of time to go the gym. If it wasn't for that incendiary scarlet gaze and the blood dripping from her teeth, I'd have hit that. Now I'd hit it for a whole different reason.

"I'm gonna say no."

She was not alone. I could see silhouettes in the smoke, dozens at least.

"What the actual—?" Martinez breathed.

Gunny cut him off.

"The fireworks back in HQ... must have drawn them in."

"Marines," I said, dread digging into my spine with icy fingers as more and more silhouettes loomed out of the smoke. "Into the trucks. *Quietly.*"

Mutters of "kill" and "errah" came back to me. Alpha Squad jammed mags into their carriers and the SAW gunners grabbed boxes for their 249s, feeding the chained ammo into their weapons.

"What's the word, Corporal?" PFC Sanchez asked CPL Sloane. She was SAW gunner for 1st Fireteam, five feet, four inches of pure Mexican firewater. She looked tiny next to her weapon, but she was good with it. "What condition we at?"

"Oh, we are absolutely at Condition One, Sanchez," Sloane said, glancing at me as he said it. I nodded, backing up his assessment. "Get that baby ready to go."

As quietly as possible, LCPL Dominguez pulled the gate to the armory open, and the Marines filed out in sticks, barrels down, their eyes locked on the growing crowd in the distance. Gunny and Sgt Major slipped into Gunny's SUV, where I'd join them once the squad was loaded up.

So far, so good.

Then Turnboe tripped. His boot caught on something as he lurched forward, and he slammed into the chainlink of the armory fence, rattling it.

In the distance, Hot and Reddy twisted toward us, her crimson gaze lighting like flares. She saw us, I know she did. Her mouth opened, and something inhuman came out of her mouth. It was a long wind-sucking howl, echoing and rebounding like an ambulance siren.

Then another joined it, and another.

"That's it!" I yelled. "Into the trucks, *now!*"

Red started for us, leaning forward into a stumbling run. She picked up speed, her arms whipping around her as she sprinted way too fast. Her legs stretched out like cheetah limbs, eating up the ground toward us.

I whipped up my rifle and fired. The shot hit her between the eyes, and she hit the deck right after. I adjusted, got my sight picture on her boyfriend running nearby, and blasted his brains onto the concrete next to hers.

The horde emerged from the smoke. Hundreds of them, all with red eyes, all running straight for us. Rifles cracked off behind me as Alpha opened fire, and the things started pitching backward.

"Slaughter!" Gunny roared.

I sprinted for the SUV and threw myself into the back seat. I shoved a big plastic baby carrier aside, rolled the window down and took a firing position.

"Let's roll!" I shouted, trying to be heard over the howl and gunfire.

Main gate was the other way. We had a U-turn to do in the middle of these red-eyes.

Gunny wrenched the wheel around and whipped the SUV into a tight turn onto the main road. All four vehicles took off, the HMMWVs' engines roaring. The swarm of freaks came at us broadside, sprinting from the grassy field of a parade ground.

1st Fireteam, with Sloane, Dakota, Marshal and Sanchez, were in the hardtop directly behind us. Then 3rd Fireteam following, with Martinez, Turner, Gutierrez, the Doc and Stevens in an old cloth top. Trailing came 2nd, with Garrett, Dominguez, Ferreira, and Turnboe in our last hardtop.

Humvees hit a max speed of about sixty MPH, and, let me tell you, it takes a while. The mob streamed toward us far faster than the trucks could accelerate, howling like banshees the whole time. I snaked a seatbelt around my leg, buckled it in and snapped it taut. I pulled myself out of the SUV window and faced to the rear, Range Combat Optic to eye, snapping off shots as fast as I could get targets. The horde hit us in seconds, covering a couple hundred yards in obscenely fast time.

I jerked on the trigger as fast as I could, sending about a half a mag's worth of rounds downrange in standard suppressing fire, but that's when it hit me. These things didn't care. They didn't even flinch as rounds zipped past their ears like angry hornets.

There was no suppressing these freaks. It was hard enough to get them to stop when they *died.*

The first runner hit 2nd's truck with a loud bang and bounced off. I swore. There had been no slowing down, no attempt *at all* to mitigate impact.

People don't do this.

Not even the goat-humping Taliban slammed their bodies full tilt into armored trucks.

He wasn't alone.

Two, three, a dozen slammed into the HMMWV, actually knocking it to the side. Ferreira wrenched the wheel back and forth, trying to keep the truck stable. I fired non-stop, not even trying to kill the things anymore. My shots ripped into their knees, thighs, anything that might trip them up. 2nd Fireteam's truck accelerated, crazed freaks hanging onto the windows with their blackened fingers even as Marines dumped fire into them from inside.

"Hang a right, Hudson!" Sgt Major roared, and I braced as Gunny tore the SUV around a turn. The SUV bucked as it hit the curb, but it gave me and Sgt Major firing angles at the mob surging towards us. Hundreds of them, doing that obscene howl, sprinted like Olympians after the trucks, stretching out like the tail of a comet.

We opened fire, and blood spurted from chests and arms as 5.56 ripped through them. Freaks didn't stop. I saw one guy's arm get ripped off, which isn't supposed to happen with this caliber round, and he *still* didn't stop.

1st's Humvee took the turn, and their rifles joined ours, dumping hot lead into the pursuing crazies. 2nd was pretty much swarmed at that point, with several crazies actually crawling across the top of it and reaching in through the windows. LCPL Dominguez had some outside martial arts training, and I saw him reach across, grab an arm and twist. The crazy toppled off of the truck with a scream, scraping off another three with it.

3rd Fireteam did not fare as well. The attackers ripped straight through the flimsy cloth-top cover, diving on top of the Marines in the back seat. Doc got one on him that jerked its head back and literally buried its teeth in his shoulder like it was a cougar on a deer. Next to him, two of them grabbed Stevens by his vest, ripped him out of his seat and out of the back of the truck. A crowd of pursuers stopped running to fall on top of him, and blood sprayed out from the thrashing melee.

"Sergeant! Sergeant, they're eating him!" Sloane from 1st screamed into the radio.

"Do not slow down!" I yelled back. 3rd's HMMWV swerved left and right as Gutierrez tried to shake the running horde off. I sniped as well as I could, trying not to hit the Marines in the truck while still dropping crazies around them. My fire converged with the Marines from 1st, and hot lead tore the freaks still on 3rd Fireteam's vic off to tumble into the street. Gutierrez stomped on the accelerator, probably breaking the pedal off as he did, and the Humvee shot forward out of the crowd, miraculously free of the maniacs running after them.

I let out my breath, feeling relief at the sight of my Marines making it out.

Then something terrible happened. Something awful, life-altering.

This was the second I knew the world had really, *really* changed.

Doc Ramon, a Navy Corpsman with two deployments under his belt and lots of Marine lives saved, rose from the backseat of the truck like a wolf prowling from its cave. Blood from the bites on his neck dribbled down his chest, his muscles quivered with unreal tension, but it was his eyes that arrested me.

Bright. Red.

I sucked in a breath to scream a warning, but the thing that had been Doc dove down on top of Gutierrez and clamped its jaws onto his throat. With a wrench and a twist, Doc ripped a chunk of the Marine's windpipe clean out of his neck. The last thing I saw of Gutierrez was his wide eyes, terrified and glazing as Doc chewed on his throat, before the cloth-top swung off the road, hit a hydrant and flipped over. A door kicked open and Martinez and Turner tumbled out, firing into the interior of the truck.

"Gunny!" I shouted, pounding the top of the SUV. "Turn around!"

"Belay that!" Hawke barked. His head stuck out of the front passenger side, his eyes glaring into mine.

Before I could say any of ten things or raise my rifle to shoot him, he growled in utter, bitter fury, "They're already dead, son."

I turned back, and saw Martinez and Turner stand to their feet, back-to-back, rounds cracking off non-stop into the horde around them. I watched with teeth clenched in jaw-cracking fury as the crowd leapt on top of them like animals and tore them apart.

Doc was one of them. I saw Martinez crawling out from under the cab, eyes red and mouth drooling, to get him some.

By now, we'd hit open road, and we were leaving the runners in the dust. Their frustrated howls faded into the distance. Right about then, the combat rush drained out of me, and I slumped down into the rear seat, my eyes stinging with tears, my hand over my mouth.

We sped down the road in silence for a minute, until Sgt Major said, "I'm sorry about your Marines, Sergeant."

There was nothing I could say. I'd just lost an entire fireteam, a third of the Marines entrusted to my care.

As far as I was concerned, the world was over.

Chapter 4 – CROSSROADS

Officials strongly recommend that all civilians stay inside until military personnel arrive. Under no circumstances are any non-uniformed personnel to enter the highways. Evacuation of major populations centers along the Potomac are underway, but as panicked motorists clog the major traffic arteries, the National Guard is struggling to respond to these attackers or provide assistance to those in need. Our experts recommend staying off the road entirely and...

The radio droned on. Civilians, trying to sound professional and not scared for their lives at the insanity around us. Marines knew better. Never believe the government when they say everything's fine.

"Just keep going straight, Gunny." Sgt Major said quietly to Gunny. I could see that Gunny's hands were white-knuckled around the steering wheel. "Take the 619 up to Belfair."

Sgt Major glanced back at me. "You with it, Sergeant?"

I nodded. The cold in me was starting to fade. My blood burned now, and all I wanted to do was get back and start killing the freaks that had murdered my Marines.

"Good," he said.

There's something about being a sergeant of Marines that activates on you, all the time. You spend that much time taking care of hyper-aggressive risk-takers, it doesn't turn off.

So I said, "Gunny."

His eyes flicked toward me in the rearview mirror.

I tapped the kid's seat next to me, a plastic monstrosity that took up way too much room. "Your family okay?"

He dipped his head in understanding. "They're at my parents' farm, out in the middle of nowhere in western Virginia. I sent 'em out there when I came to grab you guys."

I nodded. "Good," I said. "Lots of guns out there."

He tapped the phone in his side pocket. "Already got a text from my wife. They're safe. Thanks for asking."

"Oorah, Gunny."

Sgt Major tapped at his phone with a grimace, then stuck it back in his pocket. "The 95's jammed," he said. "Good thing they got out when they did."

I glanced around. There was nothing out here. "This some kind of back road?" I asked.

I didn't know; I wasn't from here. All I knew is we were heading west.

Hawke nodded. "Everyone's evacuating south. The 95 and the 1 are locked."

He glanced away. "Reports are coming in that the Army's shooting civilians."

I ground my teeth. I mean, I got it. Panicking civilians would overrun checkpoints, breach defenses and even kill our guys. Not to mention any possibility of biological contagion protocols.

Didn't mean I had to like it.

"What about D.C.?" Gunny asked.

We had all been thinking it.

Hawke grunted. "Dark," was all he said.

****

It took us about ten minutes to get to Belfair Crossroads. Seeing what was happening with the civilians on the 95, Gunny recommended we, being in Gunny's civilian vehicle, slide back in the convoy to the middle and let 1st Fireteam's truck be the first thing the checkpoint would see.

It wound up being an amazing call.

The first things we saw were the tanks, their massive 120mms aimed down the road at us. Marines in combat rigs and NVGs manned M240 machine guns on tripods. A single volley from any of those guns would shred our entire squad and blast the roadway clear.

And *that's* why 1st Fireteam was in front.

We slowed as we approached. Sloane had his military ID

held out of the window, just in case.

A Marine in MARPAT stepped out into the road, one hand raised to stop us, the other on his M4. Sloane brought his truck to a stop, and their heads dipped together. I saw Sloane gesture back our way. The Marine, a staff sergeant, nodded and headed toward us.

"Gentlemen," he said, peering at each one of us. His eyes were hard.

Judging by the scrape marks and blackened craters on the asphalt, along with some junked cars on the side of the road, we were not this checkpoint's first visitors.

His name tape read HARRISON.

"Staff Sergeant," Sgt Major Hawke said. He pulled out his ID and handed it over.

Harrison checked the card, scanned it with his laser gun and handed it back. "Welcome to Delta FOB, Sergeant Major."

He looked at the rest of us. "We're Condition One right now, gentlemen. Keep track of your Marines, and be ready to repel when called on."

Gunny was the one who asked. "Repel what, exactly?"

Harrison's lips pressed into a thin line. "Whatever tries to get in."

****

As soon as we passed the checkpoint, I felt it. We all did. Gunny's hands loosened on the wheel, and he sat straighter. Sgt Major actually growled in pleasure.

There's nothing like the air of aggression in a Marine Corps camp on a combat footing. I've seen airmen flinch from Marines just standing in line at a Panda Express. There's nothing like Marines activated to kill threats to the United States.

It's rage. It's anticipation. It's tension itself, breathable, palpable, thick and intense, mixed with a cold shot of icy discipline. We were breathing *Kill*.

NCOs roared across the FOB.

"Charlie, report to firing positions, south side!"

"Platoon, load up!"

"Hydrate or die, Marines! Fill those hydration systems!"

Every Marine was armed, rifles hung cross their bodies, one hand always resting on some part of the weapon. Their eyes challenged us as we unloaded from our trucks in the perennial challenge of every Marine to another who arrives in his space.

You competent? You gonna get me killed?

Mixed with, *Good to see other Marines made it.*

Immediately, security forces stepped up to us, weapons not quite trained on us. "Hold!" a major barked.

Navy Corpsmen moved toward us, each one accompanied by a security Marine. "Found the cops," Ferreira muttered, and CPL Garrett shouldered him to be quiet.

The docs moved among us, checking eyes, taking pulses.

"Any of you get bit?" one of them, a black guy named Jones, asked as he probed my neck.

I gritted my teeth, trying to keep the rage in. "Not that made it here," I ground out.

A flicker of understanding in his eyes. "So, this blood ain't yours?" he asked.

I shook my head.

"I'm still going to take a sample," he said. "That good with you?"

He was asking to be polite, but he was already moving. That and the MP behind him watching me with stone cold eyes told me what was going on.

"Are we looking at some kind of infection?" I asked.

Jones grabbed my wrist, twisted it to expose the forearm, and slid a needle into my vein with practiced ease.

"Might be," he said.

I looked down at him. "It is," I said, as intensely as I could. I remembered Doc Ramon's eyes, glowing red only seconds after he got bit.

He met my eyes and nodded. "Thanks for the blood, Sergeant."

"Oorah, Doc."

Around me, the docs finished up with Alpha. Everyone got blood drawn. Everyone got checked for superficial wounds, specifically bite marks.

I had one more question. "Doc," I said quietly.

Jones glanced back at me. "Yeah?"

I felt awkward asking. "Look, I'm not trying to be weird, but… is this, you know, zombie stuff?"

I wanted him to laugh. I wanted him to gather the other Marines around and mock me for such a stupid suggestion.

Instead, he sighed. "I really hope not, Sergeant."

I closed my eyes. "Not what I wanted to hear, man."

****

Shouting rose from the checkpoint we had just passed.

"I said *halt!*" Harrison's voice bellowed.

In response, an engine revved in the distance.

"Light it up!" Harrison shouted, and the 240s on the M1 Abrams opened up first. I dashed over to the barricade to see a civilian Toyota ripped to shreds; its engine block wrecked by a storm of 7.62mm rounds. Scarlet spattered across the inside of the windshield before it shattered.

Then the main gun fired, shaking my lungs in my chest.

The Toyota exploded into a fireball, back-blasting burning shrapnel to skitter across the road.

"Cease fire!" the staff sergeant ordered, his lips pressed into that line again. He stalked back towards us, grabbing a water bottle and squeezing the contents into his mouth.

I didn't say anything at first, letting him breathe a little after shooting what were probably Americans.

"Isn't the 120 kinda overkill, Staff Sergeant?" I asked.

Respectfully, though. You don't tell a Marine his job,

especially in this scenario.

He glanced at me, then at my Marines. He lowered his voice. "The first van we took out had kids in it."

My blood froze.

He wiped his mouth with the back of his glove. "Now, I blast them off the road so my guys don't have to know."

I dipped my head, feeling the blackness again. "Rah, Staff Sergeant," I said quietly. He spat a wad of dip spit on the ground, punched a wall and walked away.

The blackness is what we feel in Afghanistan, or Iraq. Anyplace you have to do something your whole culture taught you was wrong. Like when you gotta drop a teen with a rifle, or a woman with a vest, or a kid running at you with a backpack.

This darkness just comes over you as you violate everything you were ever taught is good and right and honorable to keep your Marines alive because the zealous bastards you're trying to save hate you because their religion's book said to.

We shouldn't be feeling it here.

Not here.

"Sergeant."

I turned to see Sgt Major Hawke standing behind me, his pitted face hard.

"They want you in the command tent. Take your team leaders."

Chapter 5 - STATE OF THE WORLD

I whistled at Garrett and Sloane and twirled my finger above my head. Both corporals jogged over to me. Together, we marched for the command tent behind the sergeant major.

"What's the word, Sergeant Major?" I asked, trying to get a sense of what was going on.

"Guess you'll find out," he said.

I sighed. "Heard, Sergeant Major."

I wasn't getting any more out of him. Sergeant majors were like hardcore dads and cartoon characters put together, brimming with Marine Corps values and canned slogans.

Then he surprised me. "I don't know, Sergeant. But it probably has something to do with you being the only Marines who've successfully engaged these new hostiles and come back to talk about it."

He turned back to look at me with those steely green eyes. "They told me to come grab you. I'm grabbing you. I'll find out more when you do."

"Heard, Sergeant Major," Garrett mumbled.

He turned back and marched into the tent.

Inside was a hectic mix of reports and comms gears. Wires ran all across the floor while hardened laptops sat on folding tables. Marines from S-6 were still working to establish connectivity for the S-2 guys trying to get to their databases. Outside, I'd seen guys setting up antennas and generators.

We marched toward a whiteboard, where an officer stood with his hands on his hips.

God help me, every time I meet an officer for the first time, he's Supermanning me. Feet spread, hips forward, chest out, hands on hips. If he had a cape, it'd be blowing in the nonexistent wind.

This guy was no exception. By the eagle on his collar and the nametape, I was looking at a Colonel Santiago.

"Marines," he barked out. As I approached, he shifted to

arms crossed over his chest. I rolled my eyes inwardly.

I'm a big guy. In terms of size, I look like a Marine. I got big genes from my dad's Nordic background and my mom's Italian temper.

So, Santiago stopped puffing up like a blowfish to intimidate me and retreated into his little turtle shell.

"Good work, getting out of Quantico. UAVs show that the entire bank of the Potomac was overrun by the enemy while you were escaping."

He looked at me. "Sorry about your fireteam, Sergeant."

Never mind. Maybe he was okay.

He looked at us. "You are now the only Marines on FOB Delta that have experience fighting this kind of hostile. I need to know everything you know."

I could feel Sloane and Garrett glance at each other. God help me, I was going to have say the words out loud.

"Zombies, sir."

Santiago's glare could have drilled through diamonds. But he didn't chew me out like I thought he was going to. Or should.

Instead, he asked, "Are you sure, Sergeant? And I mean abso-frigging-lutely sure?"

I took a deep breath. It really, really bothered me that no one was pushing back on me on this.

"Hostiles showed no reaction to suppressive fire, chest wounds or limb loss, sir. The ones we dropped didn't bleed, indicating they were already dead. Their eyes are glowing red for some reason. And I lost 3rd Fireteam when our Corpsman got bit and started attacking the rest of them. One second, he was normal, the next he had those same red eyes."

I kept my eyes locked onto his. "So, it's zombies, sir."

The colonel rocked back onto his heels and rubbed his eyes. "Should have played more Xbox with my kid," he growled.

I didn't know what to say, but he looked back towards the whiteboard behind him. It had city names scrawled across it.

"As best as we can tell, the spread started in dozens of American cities early this morning. Most likely, devices set high in the air spread an aerosolized version of this virus, weapon or whatever it is, and infected millions of Americans simultaneously. The spread was further amplified by the holiday weekend, with civilians packed together for celebration of Independence Day. This contributed to congestion of the roadways, delaying emergency response and inhibiting containment procedures."

He looked at me. "From video evidence we have from Twitter and other social media sources, it looks like the infected subjects turn feral and cannibalistic within seconds after infection. That match your experience, Sergeant?"

I and my team leaders nodded.

"Outstanding." Santiago turned back to his board. "Whoever did this turned our own population into a weapon against us."

He paced in front of the board. "Sergeant, I'm going to be real with you. The chain of command has shattered. It would appear that one of these devices went off in Washington D.C., and the last anyone saw of the President, he was ripping out his wife's throat just before the camera went dead. The VP is MIA, presumed dead. Most of Congress was in D.C. for a publicity stunt on the Capitol; the 101st Airborne was mobilized to try to evac them out."

I blinked. "Uh, who's in charge then?"

Santiago rubbed his eyes. "As of this moment, unknown. That's something that has to be worked out once we know who's still alive."

He glanced out the flap of the command tent. "We're trying to gather all the Marines we can find. I've got a platoon calling through recall rosters, but the cell towers are overwhelmed. Most of our combat strength was on July 4th holiday libo, and a lot of them were in areas affected by the infection."

My skin prickled as I realized the implication of that. "Do

we have an estimate on casualties?"

He chuckled helplessly, grabbed a remote from a nearby table and clicked it at a monitor. It showed a live UAV feed.

"That's D.C., as of this moment."

The drone feed showed a massive thoroughfare in the Capitol. The street was packed, *packed*, with red-eyed freaks. There were thousands of them, just in the field of the lens.

"Lance Corporal Jimenez," Santiago said. "Pan the camera around."

The Marine obeyed, and the camera started rotating on the drone.

Behind me, Sloane swore quietly.

It was millions. It had to be. I was looking at an uncountable number of civilians staggering through the streets of D.C. Fires raged in the buildings while cars burned on the sidewalks. Someone broke and ran from a doorway, and like a ripple in a pond, it activated the horde. They flowed toward the running meat like ants, swarming it and dragging it down like I was watching National Geographic.

It was almost worse without sound.

I felt the blackness rise up inside me again as I watched that writhing pile. I wanted to kill whoever did this to us.

Santiago glanced at me in concern. My breathing had deepened to a growl, and I hadn't realized it.

"You all right, Sergeant?"

I lifted my chin. "Yes, sir. What's the word?"

He hesitated for a minute, watching me, then sighed. "I'm gathering all the Marines we have available here for a push through to Norfolk. We had a deployment loaded onto Navy vessels there, a full battalion from 2nd Division. They disembarked and shoved out a perimeter around the naval yards. Marines are holding the line, but we need to break through these — whatever they are — and reinforce them. After that, we have to evacuate anyone who's still alive, and Sergeant, there are *thousands* of them. FEMA's overwhelmed with the number of calls from families in their basements, in their attics, and in gated communities currently under siege."

"What can we do, sir?"

He sucked on a tooth, looking at me hard. Finally, he said, "I got one for you, but you have to volunteer."

Sloane swore behind me. "Well, that doesn't sound good."

"It's not," Col. Santiago said. "But I've been ordered to detach a squad to support an extraction mission to Fort Detrick."

Sgt Major Hawke grunted. "Detrick. That's bioweapons. Who gave that order?"

"FEMA Deputy Administrator Whitney. Called me pretty much as soon as FOB Delta was established, claiming operational control over the disaster response."

He sighed. "I've got one Marine from Legal here, and he says that technically, Whitney's in charge until the actual administrator is found, someone from the executive branch takes command or the Designated Survivor is found."

Santiago leaned to look around me. "Speak the devil's name and he shall appear...."

We turned to see a civilian in a suit storm into the tent. He was white, overweight, and self-important. Classic sedentary desk job bureaucrat with a manicured line of mustache and goatee that couldn't grow longer if he tried. He had some stringy strands of hair hanging down that he probably tied into the world's most pathetic rat tail on the weekends.

Two plainclothes guards walked with him; I saw the telltale signs of weapons beneath their suit coats. Their eyes were dead as they assessed the room.

Contractors. Hired muscle. Killers in it for the money.

"Santiago!" he said. He shoved his way past Sloane and Garrett, muscling his gut through them, and looked me up and down. "This them?"

"Mr. Whitney," Col. Santiago said, his jaw tense at the man's tone. "I was just about to explain the mission to these Marines and allow them to volunteer."

Whitney squinted at us in disbelief and chuckled. "I'm

sorry, did you say *volunteer*? I thought you were Marines; you do what you're told. You're going to Detrick; discussion closed."

He stuck his face in Santiago's. "See how easy that was? Now snap to. I want them airborne in ten minutes."

The twit actually snapped his fingers in the colonel's face, and every Marine in the room tensed. The kill urge was overpowering at that point, and Sgt Major Hawke stepped forward. "You will adjust your tone when speaking a Marine Corps officer, Mr.—," he chewed on the word and spat it out, "—Whitney."

"Please," Whitney said, glancing at his guards for support and grinning. "I'm acting FEMA director in a time of crisis. I'm God on earth for you boys right now, and if you disobey orders, I'll have you shot and strung up for everyone to see."

He spat on the ground next to Hawke's boot. "Get your dog on a leash, Colonel. His bite is non-existent and his whining annoys me."

"Keep going," Hawke growled, "And you're going to find out exactly how bad my bite is."

The Marines in the room were frozen. We had instinctual dread of sergeants major, the incarnations of Marine Corps doctrine and lethality, and seeing this civilian blithely dismiss the clear signs of he's-going-to-peel-you-like-an-actual-potato was hitting buttons on all of us.

"Sergeant Major," Col. Santiago said.

That was all it took. Immediately, Hawke backed away a step and took his hand from his sidearm. I blinked. Holy crap, he'd unbuttoned the holster strap. He was about to pull down on this fat slob.

"Ten minutes, Colonel," Whitney said. "Get going."

He turned and walked out, his guards two steps behind him.

The colonel glanced at me and opened his mouth, but I lifted my hand. "It's okay, sir. We got it. Would rather go out and start shooting these things than stay here and...."

I trailed off, thinking about the civilian vehicles lying shattered by 105 rounds. The colonel nodded. "Very well, Sergeant. Get your squad squared away. Armory tent is open to you; take what you need."

"What's the mission, sir?"

The colonel stepped over to a map of Maryland. "Fort Detrick was the Army's premiere bioweapons development facility. It's been closed down a few times now, but they've always continued various projects there. I only know that because we have in our midst a researcher from Detrick. She claims there is valuable intelligence in her research facility that will help us combat this plague. Your job will be to escort her and her team so that they can collect that intel and get it back to us."

He gestured at a hospital within the fort. "You will infiltrate by Blackhawk. Fort Detrick has gone radio silent, so either their comms equipment is down, or more likely, they've been overrun."

I took a deep breath, thinking about the horde at Quantico. "What's the population of Detrick?"

He glanced at me, knowing exactly what I was thinking. "Around twelve thousand, active military and civilian personnel. Now a lot of that may have moved to other areas, due to July 4th holiday, so we anticipate that only a skeleton staff stayed on."

"Hundreds," I said.

He nodded. "At least."

Now *I* put my hands on my hips. It seemed to help me think. Maybe that's why officers did it.

"I'm going to need another fireteam," I said at last. "We need the weapons."

Santiago nodded. "Take whoever volunteers. It's a dangerous raid underground with these things everywhere, and we're still not sure of their full capabilities. Be careful, Sergeant."

"Roger that, sir."

Chapter 6 - NO GOING BACK

"So," CPL Garrett said when we exited the tent. "Zombies."

"Save it," I said. "Wait til we have the others here."

As we exited the tent, we strapped our kevlars back on. Alpha Squad stood by the trucks, waiting on us.

I halted when I got to them and took a look at my squad.

1st Fireteam.

CPL Sam Sloane, fireteam leader. Solid Marine, took orders well, fearless but not stupid.

PFC Rebecca Sanchez, SAW gunner. A little wild, a little undisciplined on her bursts, but accurate and ferocious.

PFC Brett Marshal, Sanchez's assistant gunner. Good shot, and even without deployment experience, he had held up well in the engagement on Quantico.

LCPL Dylan Dakota, rifleman and comm specialist for the squad. He knew his gear and humped more than he should in his pack.

2nd Fireteam.

CPL Rob Garrett, fireteam leader. Risk taker, Southern boy, all heart. His Marines loved him and he loved them.

LCPL Jay "Furry" Ferreira, SAW gunner. Jokester, prankster, ladies' man; one of those Marines officers hated. Hair always a little too long, just inside regulations. Looked like an undisciplined stain, but winds up being one of the most solid hands in a fight you could get. Had a real *Godfather* take on family.

LCPL Aaron Dominguez, Furry's A-gunner. Quiet, young, seemed deep. Exceptional hand-to-hand skills on the mat. The kid never lost when the squad rolled in the dojo.

PFC Kelly Turnboe, rifleman. Another solid Marine. A little wide-eyed, but falling back on his training. He'd be good, with some guidance.

"Alpha, we got a mission," I said.

"Is it hard?" Furry asked.

"She asked plaintively," Sanchez finished for him, and the squad laughed.

Even I smiled. "All right, lock it up. We're on babysitting duty. Gotta escort a civilian VIP into a bioweapons facility in Fort Detrick and get her back out. To me, that sounds like room-clearing and holding a perimeter."

"Hold up, boss," Dakota said, scratching at his red hair. "We're going inside a bioweapons facility in the middle of the zombie apocalypse?"

Sloane shuffled his feet. "That's Resident Evil. Literally the plot of the game."

I pointed at him. "That brings me to my next question. Who among you are gamers?"

Sloane, Dakota, Furry and Turnboe raised their hands. I was surprised to see Sanchez's hand go up. "What?" she asked. "Girls can play games, too."

"Yeah, and suck at them," Turnboe muttered.

"You say something, boot?" Sanchez fired back.

Turnboe straightened into the position of attention. "I did not, Private First Class Sanchez."

"Yeah, I didn't think so."

I held up a hand, feeling a little tired already. "You guys know some stuff about zombies, then, right?"

"Man," Sloane said. "Do we gotta call them zombies? Feels... cartoonish."

"Zulus," Dominguez said. "Let's call 'em Zulus. Or Zs."

I knifehanded him. "Good call, Dom. Tell me what you know about Zulu, and do it quick. We're kitting out in the armory and I need to know what to bring."

****

According to our resident experts on Zulu evil, they fit into one of several categories. You had your necromancers raising the dead, but I was reliably informed that that was some World of Warcraft nonsense and therefore not applicable to our current circumstances.

Then you had your plagues. Some kind of disease would spread and melt people's minds so that they were feral raving cannibals. That one seemed close.

Situated in the plague category were bioweapons, which were just targeted diseases. Based on what Santiago told us, this one was the most likely scenario.

On Furry's advice, we took one M203 grenade launcher per fireteam, just in case any 'Weskers' showed up. I didn't know what that was, but even Sanchez looked wary of having to fight it, so I didn't ask questions and just took the gear.

"Look, I don't anything about any of this," I said to the squad. "I watched the movies because Milla Jovovich was hot."

"Headshots, Sergeant."

I turned around to see Gunny Hudson, kitted out with a M1014 shotgun, M9 pistol and plate carrier stuffed full of shells. I cocked my head at his choice of weapon.

Shotguns for Marines are for urban clearing, used more for blasting hinges or locks off of doors than anti-personnel use. It's rare to see one in the field.

"What's that for, Gunny?"

He gave me a half-smile and patted the Benelli M1014 slung in front of him. "I played a lot of Nazi Zombies back before I had kids. Shotguns are where it's at. Those of you with M4s, make sure you land headshots; otherwise, you're going to burn your ammo for no reason."

Sloane grinned, "Yeah, Gunny, I knew it. You gotta line them up, too, take out three or four with one shot—"

"Sloane!" I barked. He jerked back.

"This is not a game!" I panned my gaze around the squad. "When one of these things bites you, you're gone. Doc turned into one of those things in *seconds*, devil dogs, so don't be pulling any stupid gaming tricks while we're out there."

"He's right," Gunny said. "There's no respawns here. There's no medpacks that will save you if you get bit."

"Sergeant?" Sanchez asked. "What about ROEs? Are we considering the Zulus people? I mean, are they Americans?"

I sighed. "That's a good question, Sanchez. I was not given direction on that point; however, the fact that no one is talking a cure means we're not. All Zulus are to be considered hostile and put down. Looks like the red eyes are an easy tell."

"Any Army guys still in Detrick?" Ferreira asked.

I shook my head. "Comms are dead coming out of the fort. We'll see what we can do when we're there."

I checked them over. Each Marine was carrying six mags in the carrier, one in the rifle. Camelbacks were full, and they had 2 MREs, extra ammo and gear related to their various MOS specialties in the pack. A-gunners carried extra ammo for the SAWs, and Dakota carried the radio gear.

"We're all qualified Expert, right?" Gunny asked. Nods all around. Marshal got a shove, though.

"What's that for?" Gunny asked.

Furry grinned. "Marshal made Expert by one point, Gunny."

"Hey, you know what they call a med student who graduated with Cs, right?" Gunny said.

"A doctor!" the squad yelled.

****

Alpha headed off to the makeshift helipad, led by CPL Sloane. I hung back with Gunny.

"You're coming with us, Gunny?"

He nodded. "Heard you needed another fireteam. I grabbed a few extra Marines, so you're already set."

He pointed at three Marines walking up. One of them I recognized.

"Staff Sergeant," I said to Harrison. He nodded back at me.

"Sergeant. I appreciate the opportunity to not do *this*

anymore."

He gestured at the broken vehicles outside the line. "I hear you're fighting Zulus; that's what you call 'em, right?"

I nodded.

"Aight. I brought a 240 team to fill out your squad. This is Corporal Solomon and his A-gunner Lance Corporal Park."

I nodded at the two new guys. Solomon was a big black Marine and Park was a little Korean guy. Both looked hard as nails. Solomon carried his 240 across a shoulder and Park had the tripod.

I pointed at them. "You good to go on water and MREs?"

Park spit a stream of dip juice on the ground and answered, "Oorah, Sergeant."

"Good to go. Welcome to Alpha. Follow them to the bird."

Gunny turned to me. "No command issue here, Sergeant. You're in charge of your squad. I'll liaise with HQ on this," he patted the extra radio in his pack, "and Staff Sergeant Harrison will command the 240 team as the new 3rd Fireteam, under your direction."

I pounded fists with Harrison. "Good to go. Let's get some payback."

I swiveled away. "Where you going, Sergeant?" Harrison asked with some amusement. "Bird's that way."

I didn't look back. "Gotta get the bags."

****

I ducked into the command tent again. Colonel Santiago saw me and jerked his finger to an adjoining tent. I nodded my thanks and pushed through the chaos.

Once inside, I saw Whitney standing in front of a folding table, blocking my view with his wide posterior. His guard saw me first and muttered something.

Whitney turned and saw me. "Didn't I say ten minutes, Staff Sergeant?" he snarled. "It's been half an hour!"

"No one gets ready for a mission in ten minutes, sir," I

said. "Your VIP will appreciate the extra time taken. And it's Sergeant."

He squinted at me in mocking disbelief. "I don't give a f—"

"Please, Mr. Whitney," a woman's voice said.

The lard bucket moved to the side, and I got my first look at the researcher we were escorting. Auburn hair, icy blue eyes, tiny, skinny, pinched features, not a lot of concession to femininity. At least she wasn't in a wheelchair.

"Don't antagonize my escort."

She rose from her seat and approached me. She was a little woman, but her eyes were blazing with... excitement?

I blinked. If I didn't know better, I'd say this chick was flushed with *arousal*.

I put that to the side and nodded at her. "Sergeant Slaughter, ma'am. Just letting you know that we're ready to take off if you are."

She extended her hand, and I took it gently to shake it. It was cold. "Thank you, Sergeant," she said. "But it's not ma'am. It's doctor."

She smiled at me with dead eyes. "Dr. Danielle Morano."

Chapter 7 - TINY PACKAGES

"Before we go, Sergeant," Morano said, "Allow me a favor."

I arched an eyebrow. "What would that be?"

"I would like to place a simple biotag inside your Marines."

I glanced at her sharply. "Say *what* now?"

She cleared an errant strand of hair from her face and gestured to the world. "We are clearly facing a parasitic bioweapon of masterful design. I require all the data I can gather to track its effect on new subjects, if I am to synthesize a counter-agent."

I glared at her. "You're saying that if one of my Marines gets bit, you want to observe the... transformation process?"

Morano leaned forward and put both hands on the table between us. "Information wins wars, is that not so?"

Again, that crazy strand of hair fell across her face, and it drew my gaze to that light in her eyes.

Understand, I come from a culture entirely different from mainstream America. The United States Marine Corps is a cult of indoctrinated warriors constantly looking for enemies to wreck. I love a challenge as much as the next Marine, which is a *lot*. I've seen Marines stacked up against impossible odds. I've seen a single gunner in a wrecked convoy clear his .50 cal and shred an ambush by himself. I've seen the ground tear itself apart in a storm of gunfire, but Marines charge through it, teeth gritted against the shrapnel slicing through their skin, slamming their chests against cover with their weapons spitting retribution.

I've seen the fire in their eyes, the exultation in overcoming a challenge.

But whatever was in that doctor's eyes was unhealthy in the extreme. She had the look of a woman with a fully activated god complex. For some reason, she thought everything happening was for her. Classic narcissist; I've seen it before. Usually only saw it in generals and some uppity colonels, along with anyone who worked for the Agency.

This kind would not hesitate to sacrifice every single one of us for her crusade, because it would be the right thing to do. And from the look of the goons behind her, they'd not feel a thing.

I nodded once, shortly. "Noted, Doctor."

"In case it wasn't clear, soldier," Whitney said, "it's an order to get chipped."

It was a struggle not to roll my eyes. Fat dude had to get his power move in whenever he could.

I did give him a death stare, though. You don't call Marines soldiers. We're not Army; the Army's the Army. I've served with some awesome soldiers, but they're their thing and we're ours.

A non-idiot would know that, but then again, here we were. I wasn't about to argue semantics with a moron whose chairs were built to be load-bearing.

"I do comprehend what an order entails, *sir*, and my Marines are standing by. I would appreciate any intel you have on the building we'll be clearing for you."

Morano smiled at me. "Absolutely. Thompson, the map, please?"

One of the goons moved forward. He was a big, blue-eyed blonde; master-race type. I could see in his eyes how disposable he thought I was.

Typical merc. I ran into them all the time in Afghanistan, and it was a toss-up as to whether I wanted to shoot them or the hajjis more.

"Here you go," Thompson growled at me, tossing a cylinder at me. Inside was a rolled-up map.

I touched it to my forehead, holding eye contact with him. "Thanks."

****

"This thing fricking hurts," Ferreira whined, scratching at his arm as the Blackhawk choppers powered through the air.

I didn't answer, but he was right. It did fricking hurt.

Whatever Morano had injected into us went into our upper arms, like those diabetic monitors. It had been big, too; my tricep would ache for days.

I didn't answer because I was too busy staring at the new world we lived in. Columns of smoke rose everywhere, reaching into the sky in billowing clouds. Even over the heavy drum of the chopper blades, I could hear car alarms going off, horns, sirens.

Worst of all, in the trees beneath our feet, I saw shadows running, leaping. Thousands of red eyes turned up when they heard our choppers, and I could see them gleaming in the darkness below the trees. Hordes of them streamed after us, unable to keep up but still trying.

It was hard to believe we were still only on Day One of this nightmare.

Something sparked off the side of the chopper, and the pilot shouted, "Hang on!"

Me and 1st Fireteam had already grabbed the loops on the Blackhawk when he jerked the stick to the side in a steep bank.

"What was that?" I said into my headset.

"Small arms fire," the pilot answered. "Civilians want us to go get them."

"By shooting at us?" I asked incredulously.

I saw the pilot's lips go thin. "They think we can't hear 'em," was all he said.

I settled back into my seat, feeling darkness again. "Got it."

Our flight path took us over the woods of Virginia to cross the outskirts of Washington D.C., and I have never seen a more dystopian vision of Hell. Fires already raged across the city, and even over the chopper blades, I could hear that demented howling.

"Sergeant," Ferreira said through the headset. "How many *are* there?"

Dr. Morano's voice came onto the net. "At last census, the population of the capital of the United States was 663,603. This city was one of the first hit by the bioweapon. This, of course, does not account for outlying cities such as Arlington, Quantico and Baltimore."

We flew on toward Fort Detrick in silence after that, watching the world eat itself beneath us.

****

When we got to Detrick, we didn't land immediately. We had to knock first.

The pilot hit the radio. "Detrick, Detrick, this is Charlie Two-Niner, requesting permission to enter airspace, over."

We hovered a moment, outside of the base's no-fly zone. I tensed, just waiting for a Patriot to blow us out of the air.

"Detrick, Detrick, this is Charlie Two-Niner, requesting permission to enter airspace, over."

No response.

"Proceed to target and land the birds," Thompson ordered. Short, terse, professional. He and the other three mercs with Morano carried FN SCAR-Hs with laser sights and drum mags, with extras hanging off of their black tactical vests.

The pilot's voice came over the radio. "Protocol is to—"

"Pilot," Thompson said without any tone in his voice. "They're dead."

Looking out of the side of the chopper, I had to agree with him. "We got Zs all over the place and no gunfire. They're not launching any missiles, man."

The pilot didn't answer, but the Blackhawk lurched forward into Detrick's airspace. I wondered if he knew anybody here.

Man, I didn't know if *I* knew anybody here.

The choppers touched down one after another on the

helipad on the target building, a big hospital-looking complex on the south side of the base. Chopper One dropped me and 1st Fireteam, Chopper Two dropped 2nd and 3rd Fireteams, and the last one dropped Morano, her goons and Gunny Hudson.

The howling had already started, and the door gunners on the Hawks opened up on the streets below. Their M134 miniguns sounded like chainsaws churning through a tree, and a stream of 7.62 casings fell like a brass waterfall onto the helipad as the choppers pulled away.

I jogged to the edge and peeked over. Sure enough, the shadows in the streets sprinted after the choppers.

"We got a window, Marines," I said. "Let's use it."

****

We stacked up on the door leading off the helipad into the interior of the facility. I nodded once at Sloane, and he took hold of the door handle and pulled it open.

Immediately, Marshal and Sanchez padded inside, knees bent, M4 and M249 sweeping across the hallway. No shots. I flicked a finger forward, and 1st and 2nd filed in.

It was dark inside, and hot. Must mean the power was out. Red emergency lighting bathed the interior in the color of blood.

My boot hit something on the ground, and it skittered across the floor. 9mm casing. There were a bunch of them, probably issued to security.

I glanced around. The walls, floor and even the ceiling were covered in black streaks in the crimson glow.

I keyed up my mic. "Thompson, we have blood on the walls. Remain in position with 3rd until we clear you."

The mic clicked once, his only response.

We poured through the hallway like oil. None of that stupid slow crap you see in movies; that's how you get shot. We moved at speed, almost running in a crouch, our weapons tracking across doorways and closets without pause.

"Moving. Door left."

"Clear."

"Clear."

"Moving."

We cleared the hallway in a bounding formation. As one team stopped to clear both rooms on a hallway, the other moved past them to clear the next.

It was some kind of hospital. The beds were empty, though most were covered in blood. The floor itself was covered in black footprints, some bare, some with shoes. All headed away from the central area of the floor, where the stairs and elevators were.

"Moving. Door right."

"Clear."

"Clear."

"Moving."

All I could hear was my breathing, the breathing of my Marines, the rustle of our gear and the thuds of our boots on the hospital tile. Sweat ran down my face already, and my legs were starting to feel the burn of our crouching advance.

"Moving."

"Clear."

"Clear."

"Moving."

Garrett's team took the last set of rooms at the end of the hallway before the opaque double doors. Two Marines dipped inside each room, their weapons tracking floor corner to ceiling corner, to opposite ceiling corner to opposite floor corner.

"Moving."

"Clear."

"Clear."

"Moving."

Garrett glanced back at me. "Clear, Sergeant."

I nodded. "Heard," I said quietly, then keyed up my mic. "Hallway's clear. Bring her halfway in."

I heard 3rd obey, and I nodded at Garrett. "All right. Open it up."

He took one push bar while Ferreira took the other. They glanced at one another, and Garrett mouthed, "One, two, three."

As silently as they could, they pressed the bars in, levering the doors open with painful slowness to minimize sound, and spun inside with their rifles up. Dom and Turnboe moved in immediately after, their rifles tracking across the open space. We were a second behind.

It was a large atrium. There was a big tree in the middle, because what hospital would be complete without a giant space waster. Walkways stretched around 3 sides of the rectangular building, railed with stairways leading to the two short sides. We were on the long side facing the front of the building.

Looked like we were three flights of stairs from the ground floor. That didn't bother me. What bothered me were the Zulus stumbling around the lobby area, pawing at the doors and ceiling-height glass.

Not only that, there were several on our floor. They just hadn't seen us yet.

I shot my fist beside my head in the signal for halt. The Marines froze, one eye to their RCOs, tracking targets on the ground floor. I twirled my finger around my head and started backing into the hallways. They followed.

I pointed at Turnboe, who nodded and took up position by the door. The others squatted down by me. "Numbers?" I asked, speaking as quietly as I could. I already had my estimate, but wanted to check mine with theirs.

"Fifty, sixty?" Garrett guessed. That was about what I had seen.

"Four on our floor," Sloane whispered. He met my eyes. "They do that howling alarm thing, we're screwed."

I grimaced. "Suggestions?"

Dominguez held up his hand. "I can take them quiet,

Sergeant."

We looked at him. Dom was our martial arts specialist, already a black belt in MCMAP with an instructor tab. He also had some kind of crazy outside training in hapkido or something. All I knew from messing around in the Pit was that he was *good*.

Garrett rubbed his chin. "You sure, man?"

Dom pulled out a Ka-Bar. So few of us carried those anymore. "Grandpa showed me how to use this," he explained. "He was a Korean War Marine."

We winced. That was back in Old Corps days. Those Marines killed like they breathed.

He glanced at Sanchez. "Brains, right?"

She and the other gamers nodded. "That's what kills them."

I held the tip of a knife hand to his nose. "Throats, diaphragms and lungs are good secondaries. If you can keep them from howling, that's a win."

My mic keyed up with Thompson's growl. "*Slaughter.*"

I clicked it. "Busy. Hold onto your panties."

"*Speed it up.*"

"Dick," I muttered. I looked back at Dominguez. "We'll cover you from the hallway. If it looks like you're tagged, we'll smoke 'em and fall back down the hallway. SAWs will take it from there."

Sanchez and Ferreira nodded, gripping their 249s tighter. "Good idea, Sergeant. Zs hate chokepoints."

Ferreira grinned at me. "We'll make a gamer out of you yet."

"Shut the frick up, Furry."

****

This was the day I officially became a little afraid of Dominguez.

We quietly pushed back onto the walkway around the

atrium. Without hesitation, Dom glided forward, somehow not making a sound even in boots and battle rattle. He held his knife low in his right hand, point angled toward his target's lower back. He approached at an angle, not directly behind.

I had my sight picture on the thing's head. I was ready.

Dom crouched lower to the ground for an instant, then struck like a snake. His gloved hand clamped around Zulu's mouth, just as his blade punched up under its chin. The Z spazzed, its arms seizing, but Dom twisted the knife with a brutal jerk and the thing collapsed, limbs jerking. Dom caught it and gently laid it to the ground, pulled the blade from its skull and wiped the blade clean.

Then he shot me an actual thumbs up.

"Holy *sh*—" Garrett muttered, and I clenched my fist at him to shut up.

The next Z knelt about a dozen paces away, back to Dominguez. It was picking at something on the ground.

Dominguez slammed the tip of his knife into the base of its skull and wrenched it around, again muffling the thing's mouth.

A minute later, all four Zulus lay dead on the ground and Dominguez padded back to us like a panther.

"Clear," he said, and squatted down next to us.

"Clear?" Garrett asked, dumbfounded.

"Dude, they're totally making Mexican *Assassin's Creed* after this," Dakota whispered, and grins flashed all around Alpha.

"Good to go," I mouthed. "Let's find a way downstairs."

Chapter 8 – ZULU TIME

With the hallway and the floor cleared, SSgt Harrison brought Dr. Morano and Thompson's crew up. She knew the facility better than we did, and the mercs had studied the layout extensively. While Solomon and Park covered the nearest stairwell with their 240, Thompson laid out the facility map and pointed at the stairway at the end of the east hallway.

He tapped it once, moved to the first-floor diagram where the stairwell exited out, then traced his finger down for about thirty yards to an elevator.

He glanced at me and mouthed, "Underground."

I winced and signed back. *No power.*

He smirked like I was stupid. *Generator below.*

I glared at him.

Fine.

We just had to sneak twenty people around a massive horde of zombies.

****

The doors to the east hallway were already jammed open, probably when the choppers arrived. Looked like most of the Zs had moved that way, following the noise of the rotors and leaving us an empty hallway.

"Sergeant," Sanchez whispered.

I scooted closer to her and put my ear next to her mouth. "Watch out for trapped ones," she said. "They can't open doors, so if they get stuck and we open their door, they're gonna jump on us."

Great. Now we had to watch for ambushes in an unknown environment. This zombie crap *sucked.*

"Heard," I muttered, and moved off. In a series of rapid-fire gestures, I assigned 3rd to cover our backs, while 1st and 2nd moved on clearance.

We shuffled down the hall at speed, weapons twitching around corners. There was no way this luck would hold, and I could feel my Marines tensing at the continued fortune.

Fortunately, if there was anything that made Marines frosty, it was passing an inordinate amount of time without getting violated by the Great Cosmic Green Weenie. We knew the other shoe would drop, and we just braced for impact.

****

Sure enough, the Weenie did not disappoint.

We sent our pet ninja into the stairwell first, piling after him with rifles cocked and locked. He slammed his knife under the chin of a trapped Zulu and wrenched it around while I slammed the butt of my rifle into its forehead. The thing collapsed with a wheezing gasp.

"Move," I growled, and we did.

Our boots rang off the steps, no matter how we tried to cushion. I figured all the Zulus that could were at that big glass front, still trying to follow the choppers. Sweat stung my eyes, and I swiped at my eye line with my sleeve.

Double metal doors at the bottom, that cheap tan color the military seemed to love so much. I scanned the hallway through the narrow vertical window; seemed clear.

As gently as possible, we eased the push bar in and slid into the hallway.

So far, so good. Which is what the dude falling forty stories said on every floor til the last one.

The elevator we wanted was on our side of the hall. The corridor itself was as trashed as the others, equipment scattered across the floor with torn bedding and sprays of blood everywhere. I was starting to notice the smell, too; stale air mixed with the iron stench of blood and some other bodily fluids.

As soon as Morano's team exited the stairwell, I held up a fist for halt. All eyes fixed on me. Slowly, I tapped a broken monitor on the ground with the toe of my boot. It gave a tiny squeak on the floor.

Nods all around. They would check their feet to reduce noise.

I pointed to the elevator, and held up two, then three fingers. 2nd and 3rd would set up fire lanes around this elevator shaft; according to Morano's goons, it was the only way in or out of the secure underground facility.

Harrison's Marines immediately dropped the tripod for the 240 they were carrying and trained it down the hallway. They had it up and Condition One in under sixty seconds. Park set up all his ammo cans from his pack next to the weapon system.

2nd fireteam set up on either side of the 240, careful not to obstruct its lane.

Growls surged down the hallway, and we froze. The sound persisted for a few seconds, then subsided.

I glanced at Gunny.

He nodded back, pantomiming a deep sigh of relief.

I gestured to Morano's team. 1st Fireteam and I would descend with them to secure the elevator. Morano scooted forward, her little lab coat blowing around her, and she rapidly tapped out a code sequence into a non-descript keypad by the door.

Ten seconds later, the elevator dinged.

It actually *dinged* like it was 1973.

All the low-level snarling halted for a single frozen second, then the Howl started. The same mind-shattering ululating gasp ramped up to ten blasted down the hall and I saw the first red eyes lock onto us as feet pounded the tiles.

"Well, stealth is over," I said. "Weapons free, Marines; headshots if you can. Ferreira—"

He glanced at me, hefting his 249.

"Fire when the 240 reloads."

He nodded. Last thing we needed was both squad weapons down at the same time.

The zombies poured into the hallway like a screaming

flood as the elevator doors opened.

"Get in!" I barked at Morano's team, just before the 240 opened up and we stopped hearing things.

In an enclosed space, the roar was deafening. It completely swallowed the howl of the Zulu tribe, drowning them out in a deafening *thud-thud-thud* that threatened to pop our eardrums.

It popped more than eardrums on the Zulus.

Marine Corps machine gunners are trained to fire in bursts. It allows them to stay on target and preserve as much ammunition as possible. Generally, you hold the trigger for the duration of "Die, fuzzy bunny, die."

CPL Solomon's first DFBD chopped into the front ranks of Zulus. Black blood and chunks of flesh blasted from their chests and abdomens, staggering the things.

None of them dropped. They kept coming, thirty yards away.

"*Headshots*, I said!" I shouted.

Harrison nodded and the barrel tracked up a tick.

The second fuzzy bunny went out. This time, heads popped like rotten cherries and six or seven Zs dropped, tangling the legs of the ones behind.

"Frag out!" Gunny yelled, and every Marine present clapped hands over their ears just before the frag round chunked out of his underslung M203.

The round arced above the Zs heads, Gunny Hudson's placement expert in the extreme. It impacted on the overhead frame of double doors bisecting the hallway, right in the middle of the onrushing horde, and detonated.

I could feel the *thoom* in my chest, and my body tensed, ready for the shrapnel to rip through my flesh.

But Gunny knew what he was doing. The mass of the horde absorbed the pressure wave and shrapnel. Zombies hit the deck in droves, those closest to the blast shredded into organic tatters while those further out slumped to the floor, their rotten brains pulped to jelly.

I glanced at Hudson and he shot me a thumbs up. "We got

this, Sergeant," he shouted. "We'll hold here."

I tapped my radio. "Stay on comms."

He nodded, snapped his shotgun to his shoulder and capped a Z at twenty yards. The blast lifted the runner from its feet and threw it backwards into the horde.

"Alpha Squad," I shouted.

"Sergeant!" came the answer.

"What do we do?"

"Kill!" Alpha roared.

I slipped into the now-packed elevator, trying to lever my body and weapon in next to Thompson's massive shoulders. My chest felt tight, leaving half my squad here, but the mission had to come first. Harrison and Hudson would take care of my Marines.

It was time to see what Morano knew.

Chapter 9 - WOMB OF HELL

As the elevator descended, we could still hear the gunfire holding steady above us. I'd been in firefights in Fallujah, Kabul and countless villages out in Afghanistan; I knew how to tell disciplined fire from panicked, and the bursts I heard above me were measured. Alpha was fine.

I put them out of my mind and put my head in the game. Sanchez's warning popped up in my memory, and I muttered, "Watch it when the doors open, Marines."

1st glanced at me.

"If any of those things are stuck down here," I elaborated. "Then the party upstairs is driving them wild. Get your NVGs on; get ready to sweep the facility."

Thompson grunted. "Your team holds the elevator," he rumbled. "Don't go wandering anywhere else."

I glared at him. "Don't give me orders," I said. "We'll do our jobs, whatever that takes, without any input from hobbyists."

The big guy shouldered me in the cramped confines, slamming my head into the metal doors of the elevator. His voice took on a deadly edge as he snarled in my ear, "You're not cleared for this floor, ground pounder. *My* team will sweep the labs. Babysit the elevator, stand by for our return. Be found anywhere else, and I will take action. No one's gonna notice a couple extra jarhead biters staggering around. Have I made myself clear enough for you, Slaughter?"

I took a breath, let it out slowly and lifted my head off of the door. I twisted around to look him in the eye. "Aye, aye, douchebag. Sanchez, there will be no problems, as we are upstanding Marines and citizens, aye, Sergeant?"

Sanchez grinned. "No problems, aye, Sergeant."

A growl rose from the Nordic giant's chest, and I could smell the violence rising. Homeboy didn't like being mocked. Good. My blood was rising, too, and I was itching for a reason.

Just give me an excuse.

Sadly, it was not to be.

"That's sufficient, Mr. Thompson," Dr. Morano said, interceding before the two of us killed each other right then and there. "I'm sure Sergeant Slaughter understands his role here."

Thompson glanced at us with those dead shark eyes of his, but surprisingly, instead of pushing the situation, he eased back and said, "Yes, ma'am."

His hand rested on his SCAR, and his eyes had that amused cast to them all of a sudden as he smirked at some kind of inside joke. Really, really didn't like the implication there.

Then the elevator started to slow and I shoved it out of my mind.

I could already hear hands clawing at the door.

****

The stupid cliched thing dinged again and the doors split open, admitting a forest of grasping limbs. Red emergency lighting bathed the hall beyond, and dozens of pairs of crimson eyes lit in the black. The howls and snarls surged to a cacophony as soon as they caught sight of us.

As soon as I fit through the crack of those opening doors, I exploded out of the elevator into the middle of them. I swept their hands aside with my rifle and shoved them all back, staggering the horde. I then ducked and clapped my hands over my ears just as 1st Fireteam opened up behind me with their weapons. Fire spit above me, and my covered eardrums still shook with the thunder of automatic and semi-automatic fire. I kept my eyes and mouth closed, and brains and blood spattered on my back with Marshal, Sanchez, Sloane and Dakota's coordinated fire blasting the Zulus point-blank.

The first volley scythed down the crowd just outside the elevator, clearing everything around me. With all of them focusing on me, that protected our cargo in the elevator. Now we could clear the rest of the room.

I spun on one knee, rising again as the closest Zs fell backwards, got my sight picture on the black strip between red eyes and started putting 5.56 there. With my precision fire and Sanchez's 249, we cut the crowd of twenty or so down to scrap parts in seconds.

With the first threat gone, I pulled down the monocular folded up on my kevlar over my left eye. The world went half green and showed infrared lasers stabbing into the darkness.

Zero movement.

I swept the area as 1st fanned out behind me. "Clear," Dakota whispered, and Marshal and Sanchez echoed him.

"Clear, Sergeant," Sloane said to me, and I turned back to Thompson and his team.

"Clear. How long do you need?"

Dr. Morano stepped out past Thompson. She did not seem at all fazed by the organic shrapnel glazing the floor. That kinda bugged me, too.

"No more than five minutes, Sergeant."

Thompson chucked his chin at his team, and the four brutes filed out of the elevator, SCARs raised and green laser beams already active. Thompson shouldered past me with an amused grunt, and I had to fight not to shoot him in the calf.

"Stay," he said, still with that smirk. "Play dead."

As the contractors moved off, I shook my head to clear it. That freak was getting to me.

I felt Sanchez shift next to me. "Man, Sergeant," she said. "I thought you were going to pop him."

I shrugged and cracked my neck. "It's all right, Sanchez," I said. "Maybe something will eat him."

Sanchez grimaced. "Do these things eat creatine?"

"Not like he does," Marshal deadpanned, and we chuckled.

****

"Golf Sierra Hotel, this is Sierra Sierra, how read?"

I released the call button my radio and waited. We were deep underground, something like thirty floors, if I remembered right. We couldn't hear any gunfire, but that didn't mean there wasn't any.

I got no response.

"Too far underground," Sanchez muttered, and I nodded.

"Just checking," I said.

It sucked just waiting in this weird lobby, whatever it was. I'm not made for inaction, and the tension was getting to me. I checked the area for the hundredth time in two minutes. Still just a weird plastic plant in the corner, a couple of black chairs with vinyl upholstery complete with blood spatter and bullet holes, and the required pictures on the wall of the chain of command.

We could hear echoes of gunfire from Thompson's team. Their silenced SCARs coughed more than barked, but if you knew what to listen for, it was pretty clear. Growls and howls would cut off almost immediately, and I never heard the telltale chatter of panicked fire. Grudgingly, I had to admit they seemed like they knew what they were doing.

Of course, they'd probably been capping ISIS leaders and their kids black-ops-style before all this, so they were right at home underground shooting weaponless civilians in the dark.

I checked my watch. Six minutes.

"They're late," I muttered, shifting my stance.

Sloane shrugged. "No plan survives contact with the enemy?" he offered.

"There might be a plan," I growled. "I'm just not sure we were let in on it. Stay here."

Sanchez glanced at me, the eye not covered by an NVG monocle concerned. "You sure, Sergeant?" she asked. "They were pretty clear about us not seeing their toys."

I cracked my neck. "It'll be fine. What are they going to do, court-martial me?"

"You're gonna get in trouble…," Sloane muttered sing-song.

"I'm a thirteen-year sergeant, corporal," I said, cracking my neck. "I been in trouble."

I tucked my rifle stock into my shoulder and stepped off.

After a few seconds, I heard Marshal say, "Hey, if you think about it, it's a good time to be a necrophiliac, right?"

I heard a very feminine groan, then a, "Shut up, Marshal."

I grinned and moved into the underground of Detrick.

****

It was cold down here. Power might have failed elsewhere, but Morano's little kingdom must have had its own generator backups. The main lights were still off, though, leaving the sterile white hallways bathed in a red glow.

I say sterile; I mean austere. With all the blood covering everything, this place was nowhere near sterile.

The underground facility was a maze, a network of non-descript hallways with doors spaced every twenty or thirty feet. There were no names on the doors, just a letter with two numbers after it. I was seeing B17, B18, etc. Probably had something to do with confusing intruders, and it was working. I had no idea where I was, and I had to keep a running mental log of what turns I had taken so I could get back.

Long glass windows let me see in some of the rooms. Some had banks of computers, all shattered beyond repair. In one, I saw a broken keyboard and little plastic keys scattered across the floor, next to a pair of motionless legs hidden by a desk. Dried blood exploded from around the corpse, and I winced as my mind immediately started animating that encounter.

Others had surgical tables in the center, cameras in the corners, sinks along the wall and drains in the floor. Tools and instruments scattered across the bloody tiles, and I could see scratches on the doors, showing where the staff down here had tried to hold the doors against the Zs outside.

What I couldn't figure out is how Zulu had made it down

here in the first place.

If this had been an airborne contagion, it should have hit the whole floor simultaneously through the A/C system. Like I said before, it was cold down here. The system was clearly working.

So how were people fighting for their lives to hold a door, if they'd all been infected at the same time?

Something wasn't adding up.

I ducked through the rooms, silent as a shadow. I took care not to disturb anything; I didn't need Thompson's team hearing movement and taking shots at me.

I saw Zulus scattered around the facility, heads shredded by 7.62 rounds. These Blackwater types loved their SCARs, since it was easier to source NATO rounds internationally. Looked like they were using the thirteen-inch barrels, too; better for close-in and urban fighting. I didn't hear the coughs of suppressed automatic fire anymore. They must have cleared their AO.

I stayed tense and locked in. Those guys were here to escort Morano, not clear the floor. If there was a Zulu trapped somewhere, I didn't want it catching me with my pants down.

The Zs themselves were dressed in military uniforms or lab coats. Looked like a mix of Army and civilian personnel. The faces looked… strange, though; different than I expected. Cheeks entirely sunken in, skin stretched to paper thickness, red eyes bulging. They seemed *more* rotten than the ones we'd already dealt with upstairs.

Scattered around them were bodies that weren't Zs. The scatter pattern of the corpses indicated they died running.

I knelt next to one. Her throat had been ripped out and from the ground meat of her shoulders and belly, something had been feeding on her. No red eyes, though. Must have died before infection.

I checked the next one. This one had bullet wounds in the chest and neck, entering the back and exiting out the front.

I frowned. That looked like friendly fire, which is

understandable enough in this kind of chaos. But from the direction they'd fallen, they looked like the fire came from the direction Morano and her team had just entered.

That bugged me. I didn't know why it bugged me, but I let it bug me. I was certain the more I saw, the more the problem would untangle in my mind.

I glided through the hallway, hugging the wall but not too close. If the contractors opened up on me, I didn't want to risk missed shots skipping along the wall and hitting me.

Speaking of the wall....

I stopped for a couple of seconds, staring at it. The white plaster had deep grooves dug through it, in random patterns. One of these things had been swiping at the wall with its fingertips.

Trying to dig out?

That couldn't be right. Wasn't deep enough for digging. This looked more like... boredom.

I'd seen this kind of thing before, but from Marines. If Marines got bored enough, they started decorating everything in dicks. Porta-johns in the field, especially; covered in cartoon penises.

That also bugged me. Everything I had seen so far indicated that these things were absolutely braindead. They ran straight into automatic weapons fire, for instance.

So now one of them was wandering around down here, stuck, and swiping at the wall because it was bored?

Don't like that. Really don't like that.

I moved on, the hairs on the back of my neck tingling.

Doorway to my left, dark. I pied the corner through the door, meaning I stepped around it, sweeping the room with my rifle checking all possible places an enemy could be hiding. My eyes adjusted quickly, and I saw a lot of things in a couple seconds.

First, two Zs sprawled across the floor, clearly dead with fresh blood patterns sprayed behind them. There were what looked like glass enclosures on the far wall, or more likely really thick plastic, hosting said blood patterns. I'd seen cages like that in zoos, so people could see the animals in their enclosures. Their doors were open, and the dead Zulus lay just outside those doors. From the spacing and placement of the bodies, they'd been inside those enclosures. Merc team must have let them out and capped them immediately.

Second thing I noticed was that inside those — pens — were some kind of capsules set on a table. They looked the same as the CS pellets the Corps used for annual gas chamber training. I glanced up at the corners, and sure enough, there were a couple cameras angled down at the pellet.

I had a real bad feeling, so I looked at the Zs again. They were wearing convict orange with numbers on their backs.

Felons in cages, turned to Zs, let out and killed by Morano's goons. Gas capsules, but no gas masks.

Oh, man.

Finally, my brain identified the acrid stench standing out from the sick sweet smell of rotten flesh: kerosene. The room had been doused in accelerant. Only one reason to do that.

This isn't a retrieval op. This is clean-up.

Worse, the Zs had the same extent of decay as the others down here, if not more. Definitely more than two days, which shouldn't be true, since this was all supposed to have started yesterday, right?

"Crap," I said quietly.

I saw something white on the grey flesh of one's arm. I approached quietly, my rifle aimed straight at its skull, even though it already bloomed open, red and raw. I didn't think a Z could evolve immunity to headshots, but I wasn't taking any chances. I was already living in a freaking video game as it was.

I nudged it with the barrel. Nothing.

I reached down and checked the white square. It was a medical tag, reading *Subject D-14*. It was on the exact same location as the tag Morano had put in us.

"*Crap*," I muttered.

"See anything you like, meat?"

Thompson's voice growled out of the blackness. I twisted around, but managed to keep my rifle barrel down.

"These were in cages, weren't they?" I asked, even though it wasn't a question that needed an answer.

Thompson's eyes were cold in the dim emergency lighting. "Get back to the elevator. You're not cleared for this facility."

Yeah. Yeah, I definitely wasn't. Especially since I had just found out that all of this had started here.

Chapter 10 - SCARS

We glared at each other for a few seconds. I could feel the tension in my body, the go-time energy pooling in my muscles.

I didn't bother asking questions; neither did he. I'd seen stuff I wasn't supposed to see. Learned stuff I wasn't supposed to know.

The muzzle of his SCAR wasn't picking up yet, but his fingers curled around the grips. He was thinking it.

That's okay. If he wanted a showdown between rifles, that was something I could handle. I let out a breath slowly, and Thompson lifted his chin at the sound. He smirked at me, and I saw his muscles tense.

Just before I made the call to shoot first, Thompson's mic blurted, *"Boss?"*

Neither of us moved, still watching the other.

I tilted my head toward his radio. "You gonna get that?"

Slowly, not taking his eyes off me, Thompson tapped his ear. "What?"

Nothing in my radio. Great. They're operating on a separate channel, too.

I have good ears, despite all the firefights I've been in, and Thompson had his volume turned up too loud in his earpiece. Must have been too good for ear pro when he was in.

"Smart one's still here, boss. Looks like it's circling the doc. She thinks it's Franz."

Thompson's face went grim and he straightened. He glanced at me. "Get back with the other dogs, meat."

He strode out of the cage room, two fingers to his earbud. "If he's still here, he's pissed. Keep on the doc and...."

His voice faded out.

I stared after him, trying to come to terms with what I'd just discovered and hard. My pulse pounded in my ears at the implications.

What on God's green Earth is a 'smart one?'

Against my better judgment, I elected to do what Thompson told me. I double-timed it back to Alpha, not bothering to clear the rooms I passed. If something jumped out at me, I'd rip it apart.

My mind blazed with fire. Thompson hadn't been hunting me. He'd been hunting this smart Zulu, the one called Franz.

I burst back into the lobby, calling out, "It's Slaughter; don't shoot!"

Sloane, Marshal and Sanchez lowered their weapons. "Sup, Sergeant? Find anything cool?" Marshal asked, but I ignored him.

I moved to the wall, where the pictures of the ranking brass showed on the wall. I jumped past President, Veep, SecDef and base commander down to the last picture on the wall.

Colonel Franz, head of USAMRIID, the Army's infectious disease research division.

I pointed at the picture. "You guys seen a Zulu that looks like this guy?"

Sanchez shook her head. "No, Sergeant."

Marshal echoed her, but Sloane, a weird tone in his voice, asked, "Is he your height, wears his rank on his scrubs and sways in the shadows like a super creep?"

That was way, *way* too specific. Without hesitation, all four of us whipped our rifles up to aim behind me and spat gunfire. 5.56 streaked through the air but hit nothing. With a howl, something dark and huge blurred back into the black hallways of the facility.

I surged forward to give chase, but Sloane called out, "Sergeant!"

I hesitated and glanced back. Marshal and Sloane had backed into the elevator car. Marshal boosted Sloane up, who reached through the top door on the elevator and grabbed something. Sloane dropped back down and handed me the object.

"Telegram, Sergeant."

I grimaced. Priorities.

Loath as I was to do it, I hit my radio. "Thompson, heads up. Big Z heading your way, dodges bullets."

"Acknowledged."

That taken care of, I turned back to the object in my hand. It was an insulated metal water bottle, civilian style. I unscrewed the cap and pulled out a piece of paper.

Half out of ammo. Bird's coming back. Second wave of Zulus swarming from Detrick. Wrap it up.

It was signed *Gunny*.

I glared at my Marines. "All right, we're out of here."

I keyed up my mic again. "This is Sergeant Slaughter. The bus is leaving, Doc. Time to go."

Her voice came over the radio. *"Sergeant, I require more time to complete—"*

I cut her off. "Perhaps you did not understand me, Doctor. If we don't leave right now, we will not leave. Drop what you're doing or we will come collect you."

Silence for a moment, then her voice came back. *"Very well, Sergeant. Two minutes."*

****

Three minutes later, the elevator doors opened, and the gunfire and howls deafened us.

The reek of rotten flesh and dead blood was a punch in the nostrils. I actually stopped in shock at the devastation; Z's half of the hallway was full-on black with blood and guts. Bodies in uniforms and scrubs carpeted the floor, clogging the Zulu advance as they tried to claw their way past the growing wall of their dead.

The 240 chugged out another volley, ripping through the front rank of clambering zombies. Heads shredded off their necks or popped like blisters. These ones all had Army ACUs; Detrick's wider zombie population knew we were here.

"Barrel switch!" Park shouted, and the other fireteams stepped forward as Solomon and Park ejected the 240's barrel,

Ferreira's M249 leading. The SAW chattered, rocking the Marine's torso back, but he kept his shoulder forced into the stock and his aim on the horde. No fuzzy bunny here; Ferreira kept the trigger down and strafed back and forth across the hallway.

He needed to. There were hundreds of them, jammed into that hallway like rush hour in Baltimore. The SAW and M4s barely held back the horde, spitting fire and popping skulls, but as Zulus stumbled, it dropped their heads and made their movement erratic. It took more shots to put a Z down then, and that meant fewer of them died per second. They were getting closer, pulling themselves through a swamp of rotten flesh and the storm of gunfire.

Oh, we gotta go.

Gunny Hudson glanced back at us as we spilled out of the elevator. I wasted no time, but circled my finger above my head and stabbed it at the back stairwell. He nodded once and shouted, "Marines, pack it up! 3rd, move first. 1st and 2nd, staggered fallback. Move!"

Solomon and Park broke down the M240 in seconds, the Asian kid hiking the tripod onto his shoulder while the black Marine backpedaled with the weapon held low. SSgt Harrison jogged with them, checking rooms they passed for any movement.

Thompson rushed Dr. Morano down the hallway, his brute squad surrounding the tiny woman. Their packs were partially unzipped, and I saw documents, hard drives and laptops inside. I gritted my teeth, knowing what was on those drives, but I had bigger problems right now.

I stepped forward and fired twice. A Z's head rocked back with a spurt of black, and it swerved to the side, crashing into a wall and falling over. I adjusted, double-tapped again. Again. Again.

Gunny and 2nd fell back, sprinting ten yards and snapping into cover.

"Clear!"

I shouted back, "Moving!" and 1st ceased fire, sprinting down the hallway to the stairwell. At the drop in fire, the Zs surged forward.

I'm up, they see me, I'm down, the ditty pulsed in my head.

As soon as we passed 2nd, they opened fire, 3 M4s, a shotgun and a SAW blasting at the horde. More Zulus hit the deck, but they still gained ground on us.

We hit the stairwell. "Clear!" I bawled out, and 2nd picked up and ran. The Zs were a couple yards away from them now.

Gunny had clearly given them some instruction while I was gone, because 2nd ran single file down the hallway, leaving firing lanes on either side. I didn't even look for headshots anymore, I just kept my rifle at head height and pulled the trigger as fast as possible.

"Reloading!" Sanchez yelled, and the box for her SAW hit the deck. We increased our rate of fire, trying to account for the drop in pressure, but the Zs howled like they knew what had happened and barreled towards us.

2nd slammed into the stairwell, Ferreira leading, followed by Dominguez and Turnboe, tailed by their TL, Garrett. Gunny shoved Garrett through the door and shouted at me, "Clear, Slaughter!"

"Move it, devils!" I roared, and Sanchez tucked her SAW to her chest and booked it up the stairs, Marshal and Dakota right behind her. I tapped Sloane on the shoulder and he ran, his boots echoing in the stairwell.

It was just Gunny and me, side by side now against the Zs. Our weapons barked in unison, our barrels twitching from target to target and spilling zombies to the floor. His shotgun blasted three times, blowing Zulu skulls to bloody fragments.

We clicked empty at the same time, and the silence was deafening.

"Welp," Gunny said, and we both turned and sprinted at the same time as the howls of the Zs rose behind us.

****

79

The horde crashed through the door below us as Gunny and I pounded up the stairs, slamming fresh mags into our weapons as we ran. Three flights, and we did it in about forty-five seconds, humping gear.

I swore as I gasped for air, and Gunny barked at me, "Save your breath, Sergeant!"

You gotta be kidding me. Gunny never quits.

But I did what he said.

We burst out of the stairs on the third floor, the Zs one flight below us and gaining. 1st and 2nd waited for us, weapons trained on the doorway. We could hear Zs crashing into the walls as they threw themselves up the stairs to reach us.

"Frag out!" Gunny yelled, as he chucked an M67 baseball into the stairwell. As one, both fireteams turned and booked it for the atrium at the end of the hallway. The grenade cooked off and the hospital shook behind us.

I couldn't see 3rd or Thompson's team. They must have already advanced to the helipad.

The howl intensified behind us. Gunny's frag had probably bought us a few seconds, but we were humping gear and the Zulus were frenzied now, on open ground and no bodies to trip them up.

"Haul it, Marines!" I yelled.

Garrett reached the atrium first. Kid was all heart and a fantastic runner. He rammed his shoulder into the door and exploded into the atrium, his rifle up.

"Move it, 2nd!" he shouted, his foot holding the door open for us while he cracked off shot after shot.

We crowded through the door, and Garrett slammed the door shut behind us. The Zs were only a couple yards back, but he looped some 550 cord around the two pull handles and yanked them tight. Alpha, moving like we shared the same brain, slammed into the doors just as the Zs did.

"Hold them, Marines!" I roared.

"Oorah!" Alpha roared back.

Our boots skidded on the squeaky floor as we drove our shoulders into the metal frames. Multiple impacts hit the doors, but they were not coordinated and for the moment, we had the advantage of unity. The pressure would overcome that soon.

Garrett wrapped the cord around the handles around twenty times, tied some kind of complicated knot I had never seen before, threw his hands into the air like he was on Master Chef at the end of the time limit and shouted, "Five, four, three, two, one, done, Sergeant!"

"Let's go, Alpha!" Gunny shouted, and we hauled our butts through the atrium to the hallway we'd entered through.

My vision was getting black spots from the panicked running. That last hallway took forever to run down, but the light at the end of the tunnel was blinding. We could hear the chop of the copter blades, and nothing had ever sounded sweeter.

Again, Garrett was first through the doors, so they killed him first.

When the door burst open from Garrett's shoulder hit, I saw the M240. Instead of being seated on its tripod, aiming down the hallway to cover our retreat, the crew-served weapon lay on its side next to CPL Solomon's unmoving body. The big Marine sprawled on the ground, his deserts stained by spreading crimson.

My run slowed as I saw SSgt Harrison and LCPL Park, both down. Harrison, clutching at a bloody hole in his gut, was still trying to crawl away as Thompson loomed over him. The blonde merc put another round into the back of the Marine's head, blasting a crater into his skull.

I screamed a warning as Thompson's team, their SCARs already trained on the doorway, opened fire. CPL Garrett couldn't even raise his weapon before a full volley of 7.62 hit him. His chest erupted in bloody sprays just before their aims twitched upward for the headshots.

In a twisted sort of reasoning, he probably saved most of

us. Fast as he was, he'd hit the door and shifted to the side to clear the way for Marines behind him, reaching out to hold it open again like the leader he was. That shifted Thompson's firing lanes out of the hallway, which gave us an extra two seconds to hit cover before the mercs adjusted their aims.

We dived for the rooms on either side of the hallway as rounds chewed into the tile. Sanchez screamed in rage and fear as bullets sprayed ceramic shrapnel around her. Snarling, I dipped my head out into the hallway to see Thompson and his team coolly walking backwards, their rifles spitting fire at the doorway as they approached the chopper. Dr. Morano, her expression detached even as murdered Marines stained the pad in front of her, was already belted in.

The doors behind us exploded in. The Zs had broken through.

As one, Thompson and his team turned and leapt into the chopper.

I shouted "No!" and sprinted out onto the pad. Alpha followed, each screaming in fury or grief.

With yards to spare, I watched impotently as Thompson gave me the one-finger salute while our evac lifted off, abandoning us to the dead of Fort Detrick.

Chapter 11 - LEFT BEHIND

In therapy, shrinks tell you that there are different levels of anger.

There's irritated. Play a video game too long and you'll annoy your girl until she glares at you and huffs out her breath. It's like a rock in your emotional shoe; it could grow and become more serious, or you could just dump the rock out.

Then there's mad. That's bar-fight level. Some idiot disses your team, your squad, your Corps. It's a brief flare-up that passes with a good wind and you can actually wind up friends with the guy whose face you were grinding to paste.

There's anger, which lasts a while, and whatever injustice caused it needs to be handled.

But I didn't feel any of those. I felt something about fifty steps deeper down. Watching that chopper take off, seeing Thompson's smug face as my Marines bled all over the concrete, and hearing the bestial death cry of the world behind me, activated the bedrock of Hell sunk deep in my soul. Rage, black, hot and violent, clenched my hands so tightly around my rifle grip that I thought I cracked the handle.

The Zs howled, spilling out onto the pad. They dashed for us, loping like savannah predators with hands outstretched and bloody mouths gaping. They came for us with hunger in their rotten guts.

That's okay. That's how I came for them.

I hit the first one so hard, I broke its skull with the butt of my rifle. The liquid slop in its head splattered onto the concrete.

I stepped forward then, right into the middle of them. I wasn't running any more. The beast was loose, and I roared with it as I hurled zombies away with sheer rage. Rifles cracked around me, Zs dropped left and right, and I could hear Gunny Hudson shouting something, but it was all too distant around the roaring in my ears.

Hands with ragged fingernails tried to drag me down, but I shouldered and shoved them back. Zs are strong; something about their lower brain functions being in charge. But that's where I was, too, and I was bigger than them.

I punched and swung my rifle. Zs flew back from me, scrabbling at the deck to regain their feet. I hit a dead nurse in the jaw so hard it crumpled the bone in her face. I spartan-kicked a Zulu in Navy cammies and it hit the edge of the building and toppled off. I whirled around and threw another four of them to the deck, yowling in a pale imitation of the fury gripping me.

I hammered them. I punched, kicked, elbowed, stomped and ripped them. My Marines had been betrayed and murdered by monsters that looked like humans, and these things were going to supply the first of many down payments on that debt. I took it from them in blood and bone, dropping them in broken heaps on the helipad. I consecrated the fallen 3rd with showers of zombie gore.

There were too many of them. The analytical part of my brain knew that, but it had no sway on what decisions I made. I just stepped into them. The howling of the Zs was no match for the howling in my skull.

I would have died there. I *wanted* to die there.

Gunny Hudson saved me.

"Marines, *now!*"

Rifles barked behind me. The Zulus just in front of me dropped or staggered backward. Then the frags exploded. Black blood and body parts showered over me, and I stumbled from the blasts. Then Gunny Hudson's arm wrapped around my throat, and I choked at the sudden crushing pressure. He hauled me toward the low wall on the roof, not letting me regain my balance. I thrashed in his grip, reaching for the Zs even as they clawed for me.

The man did not warn me or even hesitate. He just threw me off the roof.

I shouted in panicked shock as I hurtled toward the ground,

but then my pack straps snatched me by the shoulders about three yards from impact. I spun in the air and smashed into the side of the hospital, dazing me.

Beside me, Marines rappelled or slide down the side of the building.

"Cut him down!" Hudson roared, and something heavy smashed into my back, driving the wind from my lungs.

"Sorry, Sergeant. Don't kill me, please," Dakota said. Something snapped above me, the tension in my shoulders vanished and I fell again.

This time, I hit the ground with Dakota on my back, and I just managed to tighten my core before the air blasted out of my lungs again.

"Move it, Alpha!" Hudson barked, and I staggered to my feet. The fall and the impact had shocked the rage out of me, and I followed Hudson's orders on instinct, my mind reeling.

Something smashed on the ground next to me with a wet crunch. I jerked away from it, and saw a broken Z in a doctor's coat snarling at me, trying to reach for me with its shattered limbs. Its red eyes blazed with unreasoning hate and it howled like a demon.

All around us, Zs hit the ground. They were hurling themselves from the roof after us, and now they thrashed on the ground with broken legs, at least the ones that didn't shatter their own skulls. They crawled toward us still, snarling and growling hungrily.

"Let's go, let's go!" Ferreira shouted, and his M249 spat a burst of 5.56 up at the roof. I ran, passing Furry as he leaned into his weapon.

I'm up, they see me, I'm down.

I twisted at the end of the ditty, falling to a knee and bringing my rifle up. I saw what he was shooting at.

On the roof, Marshal and Turnboe struggled with the Zs. They hadn't made it off. They were pinned against the low wall of the roof, and the baying undead had their fingers hooked in the molly webbing of their packs, jaws buried in their necks. Ferreira fired again, and Turnboe slumped out of sight with a spurt of blood.

Agony flushed through my system, but I sighted in and fired. Marshal's head kicked to the side and he disappeared.

The rage threatened to surge up again, but Hudson stuck his face in mine. "Double-time, Sergeant!" he roared, the sheer volume and intensity of the order snapping me out of it.

The combination of his drill instructor voice and his use of my rank reset me like a fricking printer. "Alpha, on me!" I shouted, and the survivors of Alpha Squad turned to run after me.

****

MONDAY
July 4
1834

Night fell.

We jogged west along the side of some road called Porter, the Howl of Zulus fading behind us. The last bit of the sun dipped below the horizon.

We followed Gunny, our boots pounding the pavement in unison like we were on a fun run. We didn't talk. Didn't joke. Didn't even look at each other.

Each Marine felt the pain of losing a brother, the shame of not being enough. The endless rerun played in our heads, as we tried to figure out what we could have done different.

I took stock as we ran. We'd lost 3rd Fireteam *again*, along with Garrett, Marshall and Turnboe. Morano's betrayal and the dead of Detrick had cut our combat effectiveness in half. We were down to me, Gunny, Sanchez, Ferreira, Dakota, Dominguez and Sloane.

I didn't even want to move anymore.

Gunny Hudson, though, was like a machine. The man looked like an accountant, but he did not seem to tire and he pushed us hard. Sanchez was starting to gasp from humping the SAW and ammo on this run, and it wasn't some weak female thing. I was feeling it, too. We had been in two combat engagements *today* and our systems were crashing.

"In here," Gunny ordered, and he turned onto Beasley Drive. I saw the sign outside the building there; *Data Management Services.*

"Comms," I gasped, and Gunny nodded, his chest heaving.

We crowded around the door. "Locked, Sergeant," Dakota said.

It was a controlled-access door. Needed a CAC with the proper authorizations loaded on it. Made sense for a building marked *Data Management.*

"Let me try," said Gunny, and we stepped aside. He fished a card out of his breast pocket and held it to the scanner. It went green and the lock on the door clicked open.

"Inside," Gunny said, and we followed him in. The door locked behind us.

"Where'd you get the keycard, Gunny?" Ferreira asked.

"Figured the doc's team would have a skeleton key to the site, so I swiped it when we were in the chopper on the way in."

We stared at him. Ferreira said it for us. "You *pickpocketed* a Blackwater merc team?"

He shrugged. "I was a lance once, too."

"Sweep the building," I said. "We don't know what's in here. Try to stay frosty for another two minutes."

The squad, what was left of it, muttered a response. Gunny swiped us through the door separating the lobby from the rest of the building, and we moved through.

It's still a TS facility, and it doesn't contribute much to this story, so I'm not describing it to you. Long story short, the building was clear, the exits and entrance were all secure, so we holed up in a room filled with servers and slumped to the floor.

"MREs," Gunny said, as Ferreira leaned against his pack

and closed his eyes. "Calories first, then sleep. We got more to do tomorrow."

Furry whined for a second, but he dug into his pack and came out with vegetable lasagna. He grimaced as he looked at it. "I thought this was a war crime under the Geneva Convention."

Sanchez grunted. "Convention wasn't a thing yet when that one was made."

"Calories," Gunny repeated. "Didn't say food."

"Hey, Dakota. Trade you?"

"Naw, dog. I value my bowel movements too much."

I could hear the desperation in their voices. They were trying to normalize, but I just couldn't.

"I got first watch," I said roughly. I was tired, bone tired, and I still had to process losing eleven Marines in one day. "Shut up, eat your chow and rack out."

Alpha glanced at me. I could feel their eyes on me, but I turned my back on them and dug my stupid spork into a cold pack of tortellini.

Hot or cold, ash tasted the same. I leaned back on my pack, eyes on the door, and ate food I didn't deserve.

****

All I could hear now was the sound of the servers' hum and Ferreira's snoring. Kid was going to need a CPAP when he got out.

When he got out. Like any of us would.

I lay on the floor, rifle across my body, my hand still on the grip. I was looking at the door, but I wasn't seeing it.

Over and over, the scenes replayed in my head. The Humvee getting swarmed. Doc ripping at Gutierrez's throat. Harrison crawling towards me, blood pumping out of the hole in his gut. Morano's mildly interested expression, like she was watching a janitor sweep around her desk. Thompson's smirk.

My Marines were dead. I'd lost Marines before, but not the

bulk of an entire squad in a single day. I'd *never* lost that many. Things hadn't been that bad in *Fallujah*, for crying out loud, and half of them had died on our home turf in line of sight of a freaking Subway.

What did I do wrong?

I was so lost in my thoughts, I jumped when Gunny slid down next to me.

"Sergeant," he said quietly.

I nodded and looked away. I knew what was coming and tears were stinging my eyes already.

"Gunny."

I swiped at my eyes.

"You here to tell me to sleep? That it wasn't my fault? That I couldn't do anything to save them?"

Gunny sighed and leaned back against his pack. "You'd say that to them, right?"

We looked over at the lower enlisted. First-term Marines, all of them. LCPL Dakota, gripping his rifle even as he slept, just like they taught him in boot camp. Sanchez, with her abrasive feminism and Latina temper, twitching and crying in her sleep. Sloane, silent tears tracking down his face as he curled into a corner. Ferreira, snoring away like a buzzsaw as if he didn't have a care in the world. Dominguez, his fists clenching and unclenching as his nightmares took him.

"Losing Marines sucks, Alex," Hudson said, using my first name for the first time. "There's no *fixing* that. There are no words that make it all better, as if you can slap a Band-Aid on it or your mom could just kiss the pain away."

He met my eyes. "The death of a Marine is a sacred thing, and we need to take a minute to treat it as such. They volunteered for this. These kids take the worst the world can throw at them, and they leave it a better place when they go. Albeit with more dicks on the porta-johns."

I gasped a laugh unexpectedly and tears leaked from my eyes. Gunny grinned and let his head fall back on his pack.

"You can't take 'em anywhere," Gunny said, "yet they're

the greatest human beings that have ever lived."

"Freaks, whores and revolutionaries, all of them," I said.

"Geniuses and morons," Gunny responded, and we chuckled together on the floor.

We sat in silence a minute, then he put a hand on my arm. "Love your Marines," he said quietly. "The living and the dead. Remember them both, but don't let one group suffer at the expense of the other. That's all I wanted to say."

I choked in a huge, shuddering breath. "Aye, Gunny," I said.

He patted me once, then withdrew his hand. "Get some sleep, Sergeant," he said. "We're doing it again tomorrow."

Chapter 12 - HEIRS OF GLORY

TUESDAY
July 5
0730

"We need to make a decision," Gunny Hudson said, "on our next step."

The seven of us sat in the server room, digging into MREs for the calories. Water bottles and hydration packs had already been filled from the sinks.

Sanchez hesitated, her spork halfway to her mouth from her packet of square-shaped beef-inspired patty. She and the rest of Alpha glanced at me.

"Uh, 'we', Gunny?" Sanchez asked.

Hudson nodded. "We're off orders now. If we," he gestured to himself and me, "are going to continue to put you in harm's way, you need to have some input in that."

"Besides," I said, "after length deliberation, the gunny and I have concluded that you are either geniuses or morons."

Ferreira chuckled and leaned back. Dominguez eyed him. "Well, that's the closest Furry's ever been to being called a genius."

"It's one of two, Dom. 50/50 shot."

Sloane looked at me, his expression somber. "What are the options, Sergeant?"

I pulled out my phone. "Check it out. Yesterday, no one could get through to family, right?"

"Right," Dakota said. "The towers were slammed."

I was counting on him as our comms guy to be the most informed. "But when we flew over D.C., how many brand-new Zs did we see crawling around?"

"Thousands," Sloane said.

I pointed at him. "Exactly. And how many of them do you think are still using their phones?"

Dakota's head came up. "I'm picking up what you're putting down, Sergeant. You think the burden on the cell towers is lower now?"

I nodded. "So far, we've seen nothing to indicate that the Zs care about cell towers at all, so the physical network should still be up. Now, unless the whole net has crashed and there's no one left to reset it, it should still be possible to make a call out of here and let FOB Delta know what happened with us."

Ferreira already had his phone out and was looking at it with a funny look on his face. He twisted the phone around to show me. "No signal," he complained.

Dakota sighed. "Yeah, man, you're not going to get a signal in here. Data Management is basically a bunker for signals; you can't get any in or out unless you're hardwired."

"And" he said, glancing around at us, "we're technically committing felonies by even having our phones in here."

"Yaaaaaay," Sanchez said.

"Not my first," Ferreira said with a grin, and ducked as Sanchez threw a wrapper at him.

Dominguez held up a hand. I pointed at him.

"You want us to leave this building and establish contact with command?"

Gunny answered for me. "Correct, Lance Corporal. We need updated orders. I'm pretty sure that FOB Delta no longer exists and has packed up and moved. Not only that—"

He looked at me meaningfully. I took up the slack. "Not only that, but it's pretty clear that Morano and her murdering trash are in tight with the suits in charge. Even if we reported her, we'd probably just get another black ops team after us."

Sloane gritted his teeth. He'd lost Marshal from his fireteam, and it was still chewing him up inside.

I looked each Marine in the eye. "So we gotta play this smart. Even if you have a signal, you can't use your phone. Secret squirrels have all kinds of ways of tracking that crap, so no more Pokemon Go, Furry."

He put a hand over his heart. "I'll be quiet as a Pidgey in

tall grass."

"Good, I think."

I pointed at the map on the wall. It had pins in it, probably locations for servers and data centers that these techs serviced. "We need to travel south to get back to FOB Delta, if that's where we're going. However, Gunny and I talked, and we think we know what Command will do."

I pointed up and down the Chesapeake Bay. "There's a Navy deployment in Norfolk with a battalion of deployment-ready Marines. They were stuck on ship during Z-Day, so there's some serious firepower there. The way Gunny and I figure, they're going to sail up the Bay and establish a fallback point for civilians to escape. The best probable location is here."

I circled Kent Island with my finger. It was a large island to the east of D.C., situated between the mainland of Maryland and that little arm that hung down.

"There's only two bridges that access the island. A battalion of Marines can easily hold those bridges open so civilians can evacuate to Kent and get ferried out to safety."

"Hold up," Dakota said, his hand on his chin as he squinted at the island on the map. "You want to try to get there?"

I took a deep breath. "That is our most likely route, yes."

"And we can't call for an evac," Sloane said slowly, "cuz then the goon squad is gonna show up."

"Also correct."

I knew what they were looking at. Between us and Kent Island was the entirety of Washington D.C. and Baltimore.

"There's probably over a million Zs between us and the rest of the Corps," Gunny said quietly. "In infested urban environments that make Fallujah look like a cakewalk. That's why we're talking."

The Marines sat in silence, staring at the map. Sanchez kept glancing at the others, trying to get a read off them. Dakota fidgeted with a boot band in his hand. Ferreira kept smiling and shaking his head, as if the situation kept getting funnier. Sloane and Dom were silent, eyes locked onto the map, trying to figure it out.

"Dakota?" I prompted.

He shook his head. "It's a long walk, Sergeant. We going to secure transport?"

"If we can," I said. "But the road's likely jammed with civilian vehicles, abandoned as the Zs advanced. If we can find something off-road, we might use that."

"It's gotta be armored," Dom said quietly. "Don't wanna go out like Doc and the rest of 3rd."

I grimaced, hearing the pain in that admission. It was not a good way to die.

"Sanchez?"

She looked from me to the others. "I'm sticking with my Marines, Sergeant. Wherever you guys go, I'm going."

Ferreira picked up his head. "Hear that? Sanchez is coming to the strip club with me."

Sanchez grinned nastily at him. "I'm not into girly-boys like you."

Ferreira put a hand to his heart as if wounded. "You *so* don't get me."

I rolled my eyes. "Dom?"

The kid shrugged. "As long as we stay quiet, Washington Z.C. shouldn't be a problem."

"Sloane?"

He was the one that concerned me. His silence was getting heavy, and I recognized the darkness building in him. It was the blackness, the monster within that made veteran Marines such fantastic killers. But its last victim was always the Marine himself.

"Is going home an option?" he asked quietly.

The rest of the room went silent. But the Marines weren't looking at him. They were looking at me and Gunny.

Gunny tapped his fist against the ground. "There it is. The question you all wanted to ask, and only Sloane had the balls to do it."

Furry nodded at Sloane. "Rah, Corporal."

Sloane held up his hands. "Look, I'm not asking to leave. I just want to know the options here. Can I just take my Marines home and not go through, what'd you call it, Washington Z.C.? Is that an option?"

Gunny looked from Marine to Marine. His tone was dead serious. "Do you want to?"

The Marines looked struck by that. They had to wrestle with it. Dakota looked like he was physically chewing on it in his mouth.

Finally, the comms guy shook his head. "Nah. Don't like it."

Sanchez wrinkled her nose. "Yeah, it sounds weird. Marines leaving? I don't think so."

Ferreira tapped the SAW across his lap. "I jizzed six times in my cammies yesterday firing this thing."

Grins and groans broke out around the group. Furry grinned for a second, then went serious. "But Marines, like, we've never run, right? We don't, *ever*. Like, in Chosin, when we were surrounded by Chi-Coms, we saved the Army and advanced in a different direction. Or in Belleau Wood. Or Inchon."

"Fallujah," Gunny said quietly. Second time he'd brought it up. He'd probably lost brothers there.

"That's right. We do some Dan Daly, Chesty Puller-type crime and make victory happen. All I'm saying is," Ferreira went on, "is that when the world looks like it's falling apart, the Marines step up. We don't go home, not till all the Marines go home. We say no, we sharpen our freaking knives and we rip some guts out of the bad guys."

He went silent. We all stared at him.

"Holy crap, Furry," Sanchez said. "I didn't know you knew that many words."

"It was beautiful," Dominguez put in.

"Put tears in my eyes," Dakota said.

Furry slouched down. "Y'all can shut up. That was from

the heart."

Sloane finally broke his serious demeanor and patted Ferreira on the shoulder. "That was good, man. It's what I was thinking, but I didn't want do any stupid hero crap."

He locked eyes with me. "Not unless we're all doing it."

I looked from Marine to Marine. "We agreed, then? We're punching through Z.C.?"

"Right through its dick," Ferreira said, and the bunker erupted in oorahs and battlecries.

****

The plan for getting out of the building was simple. Dom had observed that the Zs liked noise. We also figured there might be some stragglers in the streets, waiting to tarpit us down so their buddies could grab us.

The particular ingenuity of E-3s kicked in.

Dakota found a battery-operated alarm clock. After a couple minutes of jerry-rigging, the Marines had it wrapped in bubble wrap like a hamster ball. He had it set to go off one minute past its current time, opened the back door of the data facility and chucked it, aiming away from our planned route of egress.

We held our breaths, listening, til we heard the distinct *beepbeepbeep* of the alarm.

"Go," I said, and we hustled out single file, running south. Behind us, the Howl started, but we left it behind.

****

Transit through the southern part of Detrick proved smooth. All Zulus in the area had been drawn by the choppers and firefights the day before, though we kept Sanchez's warning in mind about potential trapped ones.

There was an abandoned HMMWV at the southern gate, but Gunny waved us off it.

"Look at the road," he said. Sure enough, cars filled it edge to edge, spilling over onto sidewalks, medians and emergency lanes.

"Off-roading won't work, either," Ferreira muttered. "It's freaking Maryland."

Forests as far as the eye could see. We wouldn't be able to get the vic anywhere.

I sighed. "Strip it and let's go."

We found a box of 5.56 and added it to our stash. Engagements the day before had burned through about half our supply, but as long as we stayed quiet, I didn't anticipate problems with ammo.

"You know," Sloane said as we trudged along the road, "we probably don't need rounds as heavy as 5.56."

I grunted as I stepped over a guard rail. "How's that?"

He shrugged. "9 mil or .22 would do the same damage to a rotten Z. 5.56 is overkill, and way heavier to carry."

"When we get back," I said, breathing hard and swearing in the privacy of my mind, where Gunny probably couldn't hear me, "I'll let the colonel know."

"That's good thinking, Marine," Gunny said. He was walking point just ahead. We weren't spaced out, since Zulus didn't seem to be using grenades or LMGs yet, and Gunny wanted us tight just in case we had to duck down and hide.

"You keep that up," he went on. "That active mindset how your generation will stay alive in a world like this."

Sloane ducked his head, unused to the praise. I didn't blame him. The Corps wasn't exactly high on positive reinforcement.

"D'you hear that, Furry?" Sanchez said. "Active mind. Guess you're out."

"Thank you, Sanchez, for your incisive yet unhelpful comments. How 'bout you shut it before some fricking zombie finds us and chows down?"

"Nah, they don't want us," Dakota said. "They eat brains. If we had any, we'd be in the Air Force right now."

Dominguez chuckled. "I hear that."

****

We stuck to route march rhythm. Fifty minutes walking, ten minutes resting and drinking water. It made a sorry sight, the seven of us marching through the ruins of America.

The streets and sidewalks were now empty, eerie and littered with debris. No cars rushed through intersections, giving that constant background noise of moving air. Cracked windows and graffiti-covered buildings stood as haunting remnants of a society annihilated, broken to its knees in a single stroke and shot in the back of the head.

We tried to raid a Burger King, figuring something in there still had to be good. The acrid reek of smoke and fry oil drove us back; someone had left the fryers on when the Collapse hit and fire had gutted the place.

The only thing we could hear in the distance was the distant chatter of automatic weapons fire and, so faint you thought you imagined it, the Howl of the undead. Periodically, jet fighters streaked overhead, leaving contrails that crisscrossed.

We knew where they were headed. The nation's capital, a cool million potential Zs, lay that way.

We were starting to see Zulus now, ones and twos scattered across our path. They stumbled slowly on a path only they knew, their heads twitching back and forth. As soon as we saw the first one, Gunny clenched a fist and we melted into the shadow of a nearby house. The zombie didn't see us. It was too busy running its hand over a car as it stumbled along.

"What's the play, Gunny?" Sanchez asked, massaging her shoulder. She was clearly aching from carrying the SAW around all day, but our Latina fireball wouldn't complain. Not about that, anyway.

Dominguez interrupted before Gunny could say anything. "Can I try something?"

Hudson glanced at him, his eyes sharp, but he nodded.

Dom crouched down and skittered out into the street in full view of the Z. I started and shouldered my rifle, but Gunny put a hand in my chest and a finger to his lips.

Dominguez stayed in the middle of the street; his rifle aimed directly at his new friend. The Z kept staggering forward, emitting a low guttural exhale as it did.

I squinted. Why can't it see him?

The lance corporal took a loose chunk of asphalt from the road, tossed it once in his palm, then sidearmed it down the street past the Z.

Immediately, it burst to life. Its head snapped around to follow the projectile, and it lurched forward with a snarl. After a few steps, it staggered to a halt, its head tracking around, an odd cant to it.

Dom scurried back. "You guys saw that?" he asked unnecessarily.

Furry squatted, his dark eyes thoughtful as he watched the Zulu stumbling around, then he snapped his fingers. Sanchez smacked him for the noise, and he looked contrite, but he said, "It's reacting to noise and motion. Something's wrong with their eyes, Sergeant."

"Have we seen one of them blink yet?" Dakota asked, and we glanced at him.

"I mean, we've kinda had other stuff on our minds," Sloane deadpanned.

"Yeah, Dak's over here staring deep into their eyes," Furry said.

"No, he's right," I said, chewing memories over in my head. "Their eyes go red and crazed, wide as they can get. I bet they dry out."

"Yeah," Sanchez said. "Your eyes go blurry if you don't blink. You can't focus right."

Dakota looked up. "That's why we're seeing them in groups, usually. They're all moving to the same sounds."

Gunny narrowed his eyes. "That one's alone," he said.

Dakota nodded. "Yeah, but we also got jets and choppers crossing the sky, not to mention whatever animals and pets are still around. There's a lot of audio pollution in an urban environment, and I bet these things are getting separated as they try to follow whatever they're hearing."

The squad fell silent as we digested that news.

"All right," Gunny said after a minute. "Our cammies are probably actually helping us, then."

Furry sniggered. "For once," he said.

"Prioritize concealment, not cover," I said slowly. "If we move quietly, they won't see us."

Gunny nodded. I could see his mind working through the problem.

"Monkey bombs," he said.

I stared at him, but Sanchez and Dominguez both grinned. "Good call, Gunny," Sanchez said. "Looks like the game devs knew what they were talking about."

"I do not," I put in. "What the hell is a monkey bomb?"

"Sergeant," Gunny warned, and I acknowledged my slip-up with a hand.

Dom gestured. "In Nazi Zombies on COD, you can get a special grenade called a monkey bomb. It's a little cymbal monkey that draws all the zombies to it for a few seconds before it blows up."

I caught on. "Noisemakers," I said. "Like that alarm trick Dakota pulled."

Ferreira tapped his SAW. "Yeah, you know, whenever I'm running from First Sergeant—"

"How often is that?" Sanchez interrupted.

He pointed at her. "Not your business. Anyway, ignore when he calls out 'hey, Marine.' Your name ain't Marine. Then walk to the nearest building and turn the corner to, you know, break line of sight. Then freaking book it. First Sergeant's forty-five years old and busy; he's not chasing."

Gunny grinned. "Lance criminal," he said, shaking his head.

"Yeah, you know it, Gunny. But we can use that here. Break line of sight with these things, and toss your monkey bomb the other way. Might be a way to lose a crowd."

"I like it," Gunny said. "Good thinking, Marines."

He looked each one in the eye, keeping his voice low. "Our number one priority right now is to stay alive long enough to link up with other Marines. No stupid decisions, no heroics, and absolutely no gunfire unless we're good and screwed. We find our brothers and get there alive. We've lost too many already."

We nodded. It sounded good. It was a strategy, and we could follow a strategy. Stay quiet, stay hidden, stay alive.

We could do that.

Then we heard the scream.

Chapter 13 - PURPOSE

It shattered the quiet of the street, a shriek knifing through the silence. Our Zulu buddy snapped around and started running, the Howl rising from its chest in a hoarse wail. Others followed, lifting from the neighborhood around us.

We gripped our weapons, frozen. Gunny had a hand out, palm down, but he was looking around.

We heard a man's voice. "Run, Jenny! Run for it!"

A booming shot rang out. Shotgun.

Another scream. Girl, young.

"Keep running! Get inside!"

The Howl was everywhere now.

Alpha looked at me, their eyes wide, questioning. My knuckles cracked on my rifle grip.

The shift in our demeanor after that initial shock was instant and palpable. To this day, I cannot think of it without a chill running down my spine. We had just finished deciding to survive, then we heard the Call.

Sanchez and Furry hefted their SAWs simultaneously, just as Dakota, Dom and I twisted toward the yelling. Our rifles shouldered, our visions sharpened, and Alpha Squad charged out from cover like the warriors we were to bring second death.

****

A crowd of Zs clawed at the doors and windows of a house down the street. More runners loped their way towards it. Another shotgun blast boomed, kicking a Zulu back from the window to thrash on the ground. We heard crying and shouts.

"Weapons free, go loud and proud, get their attention," Gunny snarled as we ran. "We want them on *us*. M4s only. Save the squad weapons for when the crowd turns."

"Oorah, Gunny!" we bellowed, loud as we could. I skidded

to a knee as Dakota, Sloane and Dom pounded past me. I got my sight picture, and I snapped off a shot that stripped a Z's teeth from its gums before blowing its filthy head off its neck.

"United States Marines!" Ferreira bellowed, his Italian-American lungs blasting his voice through the neighborhood. "Hold fire and get down!"

The noise got their attention. The entire Zulu tribe swiveled to see the seven of us charging them, and with a screech, they swarmed for us.

I fired, tracked another one, fired, fired again to hits its buddy. Just outside my firing lane, Sloane and Dakota had slowed to a walk, firing one shot a second. Dom barged into the lead Z, halting its charge dead with a butt stroke to its face. His Ka-Bar flashed and buried under its chin, and the thing dropped like a marionette with its strings cut. He ducked the arms of the next one, swept its legs out from under it with some kind of karate move and fired his M4 one-handed into its face.

Zs pitched over backward or crashed to the ground, brains blasted out of their skulls. I heard the chatter of a 249, and I swiveled to see Sanchez chewing through a pack of five that emerged from behind the next house over.

"Get some, Marines!" I roared as undead skulls popped like black blisters.

"Oorah!" they shouted back.

Ahead, Sloane and Gunny punched through the rapidly diminishing crowd, firing constantly. They reached the broken window, where Gunny grabbed a Z by the scruff of its neck and hurled it back, ending it with a single blast from his shotgun.

"US Marines, US Marines!" he bellowed into the house, then he and Sloane burst through the door. Gunshots rang out inside.

Meanwhile, the last four Zs toppled to the ground, death rattles hissing from their throats, and I glanced at my Marines to take stock. All of us were breathing hard through our mouths, each bite of air sawing through our bared teeth. Furry kicked one on the ground and put another burst into its skull for good measure. Dom's eyes were black and hard, the killer fully emerged from its lair, and even Dakota, the one we thought of as our friendly nerd, kept tracking his weapon about, looking for another one to drop.

"Stand down, Marines," I growled, trying to get my own aggression in check. "Eyes up."

"Errah," said Sanchez, her gaze sweeping around the neighborhood on the barrel of her SAW.

"Clear!" Gunny shouted from inside. "Civilians coming out. Stand by for first aid!"

A man, woman and two teen girls stumbled out of the house, covered by Gunny and Sloane. The woman sobbed into the man's shoulder, who hefted a hunting shotgun in one hand and held her with the other.

"Thank you!" the woman gasped. "Oh, thank you!"

"I thought we were done for," the man said, his eyes wide. He was wearing mechanic's coveralls with the name *Tyler* stitched in.

I moved to Hudson. "Gotta displace, Gunny. There's no way that didn't get heard."

He nodded. "Lance Corporals Sanchez and Ferreira, flank the civilians. Corporal Sloane, take point. Dominguez, rear watch. We're moving."

"Rah, Gunny," the squad chorused, and we shifted the civilians off the street.

The woman kept crying and her daughters with her, so I snapped my fingers at them. "Hey, enough of that. These things track by sound, so lock it up."

They sniffled and nodded.

Luckily, we seemed to have cleared out the local infestation. No other Zs emerged from the housing complex or woods. About a half a mile away, we found a garage with the door slanted open. After a quick noise check and visual sweep, we moved inside the structure and pulled the door down.

Gunny turned to Tyler. "Sir."

The man wiped tears away from his eyes with his sleeve. "Tyler Garmin. I can't thank you soldiers enough. We've been holed up in there since yesterday."

The term *soldier* raised some hackles, but as usual, we didn't let it show on our faces.

"What was going on?" Gunny asked. "What drew them to you?"

Tyler shook his head. "We ran out of food. We were supposed to go a friend's for grilling, and grocery day was supposed to be today."

He pointed at one of his daughters, a lanky sixteen-year-old. "Jenny runs track in school, so when we thought they were gone, we sent her out to find something to eat."

Jenny sniffed. "Yeah, I tripped on a sprinkler in the yard and broke a stick."

Gunny looked at all of them. "So, what's your plan? My Marines and I have to reconnect with our unit."

Tyler pulled his backpack off and showed us a radio. "FEMA has been broadcasting," he said. "They're telling us to stay put if we can. They're setting up an evacuation point on Kent Island, and are gonna try and get us out that way."

I grinned at Gunny. "Called it."

Tyler looked at us. "Can you take us with you?"

Gunny shook his head. "Negative, sir. We're heading through the outskirts of D.C."

He raised his eyebrows at Tyler's family. "Don't think that's the right place to take your family."

"Yeah. Yeah, okay," Tyler said. "So, we'll just stay here, then?"

"Furry," I said. My Italian-American popped his head up. "Jimmy the door to the house and get these folks inside. Dak and Sloane, cover him and sweep it when it's open."

Furry put a hand to his chest. "I'm wounded that you assume I can pick a lock, Sergeant."

I glanced at him. "You're from Boston, right?"

"Look, the fact that I *can* do it doesn't excuse your

assumption."

"Just shut up and do Mafia things."

****

Twenty minutes later, the Garmin family was holed up in their new digs with a fully stocked pantry.

"Look," Gunny said. "You got a second floor here; stay on it. If you get in trouble or too many Zs are nosing around, head for the garage. Put a stash of food in there, just in case you get stuck for a while. Somebody stays awake all the time, understood? Looks like we cleared out most of the problem here, but we still don't know enough about these things and how they move. Stay quiet, stay safe, wait for instructions to evacuate."

Tyler nodded, his face grim. "I appreciate what you did for us."

Gunny clapped him on the shoulder. "We're Marines, sir," he said. "It's part of the job."

Tyler let us out of the front door, and as the last Marine slipped out, the door shut behind us. Several locks clicked.

"Rude," Dakota muttered.

"Guess we'll just walk of shame ourselves out of here, then," Sanchez said.

"Like it's your first," I said. "Now shut the frick up. We're moving out."

We resumed our southward trek, a line of pack-bearing Marines humping through an American suburb. Each of us had burned through about a mag of ammo, the SAW gunners being the exceptions. We had dropped around sixty Zs.

After about eight minutes of march, Ferreira said what we were all thinking.

"Okay, *now* for real we're gonna be quiet!"

Even Gunny had to laugh.

Chapter 14 - HIGHWAY TO HELL

We hiked for about four hours, stopping every fifty minutes to hydrate and ease our feet. It was relatively flat ground, so we made good time, for being stuck with our hooves.

We weren't walking on the freeway itself; there was no way we could make any kind of good time with all the cars crowding it. Instead, we used the frontage road alongside or just hiked through the woods parallel.

"We need to find a vic," Gunny said quietly as the squad chomped on scavenged granola bars. "It's going to take forever moving like this."

I sighed. "Heard, Gunny. But the 270 is still locked up."

Gunny scratched at the stubble on his chin. Sgt Major would have a conniption seeing a senior Marine with scruff on his face.

"We might have to risk a call," he said.

I chewed on that for a minute. "Maybe if we use callsigns, it won't get back to Morano? Or just say Marines need pickup at this location."

Gunny shrugged. "I imagine civilians have already tried that to get picked up. HQ's not going to send valuable air assets without confirmation of identification. Once they log into MARADMIN to check our IDs, Morano's going to know we're alive."

Ahead of us, Sloane slung his pack and rose to his feet. I checked my watch. "Hey," I called out. "You still got four minutes."

Sloane shrugged. "I'm good, Sergeant. Just draining muh wank."

"Ha! Wank!" Furry called out, because he had the maturity of a seven-year-old.

Sloane moved to the side of the road about twenty yards down, turned his back to us and unbuttoned. He did the lean to start the flow, and I looked away to give him at least some kind of modicum of privacy.

Therefore, I didn't see Sloane die.

The sound caught me first. Hard, harsh, like a table being shoved across a floor. I whipped around just in time to see a cloud of dirt speckled with grass and tinged scarlet explode into the air. Something bit into my cheek and I swiped at it and stared at what had fallen into my glove.

There was a tooth in my palm.

"Get cover!" Hudson screamed, and all six of us dove off the little frontage road. I crawled, as close to Mother Earth as I could get, mentally screaming Sloane's name over and over again.

I heard the thud of its rotors then.

I twisted and saw an Apache helicopter banking around. The chain gun on its nose whirred, and I threw myself toward a nearby Shell station. Six hundred twenty-five rounds a minute exploded at my heels, and I zagged out of the way as a line of dirt geysered into the air where I would have been.

His visibility's crap now, I thought. I had about four seconds before the dust settled.

Then my plan detonated as two rockets punched into the gas station I was eyeing and blew it into flaming shrapnel. Secondary explosions cooked off, and I stumbled in the opposite direction as the shockwave staggered me.

Something howled nearby.

"Slaughter!"

I turned and saw Gunny Hudson. He and the other Marines hunkered beneath a concrete bridge that let a creek run under the frontage road.

I booked it for them, my skin prickling as it waited for hot 30mm to shred it apart.

The rotors whined, and I dropped. Fifteen feet beyond me, a line of pavement turned into a cloud of asphalt shrapnel. I rolled over, got a sight picture, and started firing.

It's almost impossible to hit a chopper with a rifle; the

distance makes it hard to gauge the lateral movement of the aircraft. Still, it was better than dying running.

Behind me, the SAWs opened up, and this time, I saw flecks of light sparking off the fuselage of the Apache. It tilted and slid to its right, but that screwed up its aim, too.

"Move," Gunny roared, and the six of us took off.

"Into the woods!" I bellowed. We had to get this thing off of us.

It tried to stop us. It knew what we were trying to do.

A trio of rockets slammed into the woods ahead, blowing trees into splinters and shaking my heart in my chest.

Dakota pivoted, dropped to one knee and cracked off shot after shot. I saw the nose of the chopper twitch toward him, and I charged him. I hit him in the shoulder just as the Apache cut loose. Somehow, the volley went wide and we stayed alive.

"Get up, Marine," I groaned, feeling stinging all over the back of my neck from the debris lodged in it.

Then it had us.

We were bunched up at the woods' edge. We realized it just as the Apache slid to its left, its chaingun already whirring. Gunny screamed for us to break apart, but it was too late.

It was at that moment we knew we had f-ed up.

But, as they say, God loves Marines.

A missile slammed into the flank of the chopper and blew it apart in a massive fireball. A rain of flaming metal fell from the sky and crashed onto the 270, cooking off the fuel tanks of several cars trapped there, while the rotor itself spun off into the city, knifing into the roof of an HVAC shop. An F22 roared overhead, banking into a long turn and disappearing from view.

We lay frozen for a second, wondering what had just happened, when we heard a voice from the woods nearby.

"Marines. I'd expect to find *you* laying down on the job."

****

He stood in the shadow of a nearby office building. He was in Army OCP pattern cammies, with an M4 slung over his torso and a radio on his shoulder.

We picked ourselves up from the ground. Gunny helped me up. "You good?" he asked.

I nodded.

"Sloane?" I asked, knowing the answer.

He shook his head.

"Morano," I growled, and the sheer hatred I felt in that moment blanked out rational thought.

"Let's go," Hudson said. "Worry about her later. We're going to settle that debt."

The tightness in his voice betrayed his own fury.

"Quickly, jarheads," our visitor called out quietly. "We got *friendly* critters coming to see what the party was about."

The Howl was getting closer. I could already see shadowy figures backlit by the flames on the 270.

We jogged over to him.

Turns out he wasn't Army, he was Air Force. And he was from Texas.

"Tech Sergeant Jon Russell," he drawled, offering a hand to Gunny. "Air Force, combat controller."

Gunny took his hand and gripped hard. "It's good to see you, Tech Sergeant. What are you doing out here?"

Russell gestured to the burning heap on the 270. "Hunting that. Langley pulled me from leave just after the Collapse and sent me in to get live intel on the ground. Command called me up an hour ago and said a National Guard pilot with a history of disciplinary infractions and a gambling debt left his assigned patrol route a few hours ago. Looks to me like he was after y'all. Wanna tell me why somebody paid that much money to kill some crayon eaters?"

Gunny and I glanced at each other. "Yeah, we might know what that's about," I said.

Russell turned his head to the side and expertly squirted some dip spit through his teeth. "I'd love to hear that story.

First things first. Figure out right now how it was tracking you, because Apaches don't have great software on board. Somebody's feeding it your movements, Sergeant."

Gunny looked at Alpha. "Phones?" he asked.

They shook their heads. "Ditched 'em," Sanchez said.

"Anybody wearing a Fitbit?"

Those stupid things had gotten more Marines in trouble than anything. I knew an intel guy who called them the Furbies of 2015.

Alpha denied.

Ferreira snapped his fingers. "Got it, Sergeant."

"What's that, Furry?"

He tapped his shoulder. "Morano put trackers in us, remember? Something about medical data."

I closed my eyes. "Motherf — okay. Dom, got your Ka-Bar?"

Ferreira's eyes went wide. "Wait, no. No. Let's get a Corpsman. Let's find a doctor. Dude, let's at least find a *vet*!"

****

In the end, we got all six of the trackers out of our shoulders. Gunny took charge of it, slicing an X half an inch into the skin over the injection point, then digging the device out with pliers. I did him last.

Unsurprisingly, Furry whined the most, even while biting down on the rifle strap we gave him. I hovered over him, ready to muffle his noise in case Zulu took an interest here. Sanchez swore something filthy in Spanish and took a swing at Gunny when he let her up. Russell stood watch while we fished the last of the trackers out, washed them out with peroxide and slapped some bandages on.

It took about half an hour, and we tossed the devices into a puddle of water nearby.

"Let's ride, devils," Russell said quietly, and we moved off away from the trackers, away from the 270 that Morano now knew we were using.

****

"So you're a combat controller?" I asked as we pushed into the wood.

"Yep, going on ten years," he said.

Wow, his Texas drawl was strong. I was from Texas myself, but it wasn't part of my personality like this.

"Just got back from the Land of 'Stans. Was gonna kick it with some buddies on base yesterday, then got word that people were chowing down on each other instead of hot dogs. Grabbed some gear and got out here to give reliable intel to Big Air Force. The rogue chopper was just a BOLO I got. Why was that thing after you, anyway?"

Gunny filled him in over a few minutes.

The controller sighed. "Gotta be kidding me. Actual zombies, and you guys got to go see the mad scientist herself trying to erase Patient Zero? Wild. You call her in yet?"

"She won't be connected to hitting us," Gunny said. "She has a team of Blackwater types working for her. They're probably tasked with silencing us now."

"Makes sense," Russell said. "But my comms are outside of the regular chain. Let me call an airlift in and get you guys to your people."

"Sergeant Slaughter?"

I glanced over and saw LCPL Dakota. He looked tired, but there was a fire in his eyes. "What's up?"

He let out a deep breath. "We shouldn't go home yet."

Gunny heard that and stepped closer. His voice was quiet and thoughtful. "Why do you say that, Marine?"

He gestured back at Ferreira, Sanchez and Dominguez. "Sloane was talking to us, just before…."

He stumbled over his words for a second, but found his stride again. "Anyway, that thing with the Garmin family got him thinking, since he really liked saving those people. FEMA is communicating with all these civilians, right? There's gotta be thousands of them, stuck in their homes while all these Zulus wander around."

"Sure," I said. "They're trying to evacuate them to Kent."

"Eh," Russell said. We looked at him.

"What?" Gunny asked.

Russell scratched under his chin. "Well, there's another reason I'm out here. Part of my objective is to determine if evacuation is even viable prior to saturation bombing of the D.C. area."

I blinked. "Saturation bombing of civilians just to kill Zs? What's the point of that?"

Russell spread his hands. "The Pentagon and Capitol are dark; no comms coming out of them. You know how many national security vulnerabilities are in those places? If Russia or China manage to insert a team, we're going to have another giant mess once we get past this particular catastrophe. Plan is to bomb the area, possibly even using nuclear."

Gunny let out his breath slowly. "Wow," he said quietly.

Russell pointed at Dakota. "What's the kid's plan, though?"

Chapter 15 - LANCE CRIMINALS

"Here's the thing," Dakota said. We were all seated around a phone on the ground. It was Russell's.

"Municipal, county, state and federal services all have the ability to push notifications out to smartphones, right?"

I nodded. "Sure. That's how we get amber alerts, flood warnings, etc."

"Right," Dakota said. "So, FEMA has access to everyone's phones and radios now. They basically control all communications in an emergency."

Gunny nodded. "Right. They'd be able to tell the people trapped in their homes when to make for the evac point."

Dakota pointed at him. "Not just that, Gunny. The phone itself also makes a really loud fricking buzz when it gets those amber alerts, right?"

"Yeah, I hate those things," Russell said. "Give me my old flip phone with real buttons any day."

Dakota drew a quick box in the dirt. "Say this is D.C. Say you wanna get civilians trapped there over to Kent over here—"

He circled the east side of the box.

"—but you gotta get all the Zs out of the way first."

"Kay," I said. "What I don't see is how you twips solved this problem."

"Hurtful," Ferreira said. Sanchez smacked him. "Ow! Also hurtful! Jeez!"

Dakota nodded. "Yeah. Activate those phone buzzers starting on the east side, and move them west."

Gunny leaned forward, his eyes lighting up. "Outstanding," he breathed. "Really good work."

"I like your thinking, kid," Russell said. "You probably should have gone Air Force, though."

I blinked, feeling lost. "Sorry, I'm dumb. How's this help?"

Gunny pointed at the box. "Move the wave of sound away from the bridge to Kent Island into D.C. proper. The Zs will follow the sound, leaving evac routes open for civilians."

He tapped his chin. "Doesn't feel like enough, though."

Dakota nodded. "Yeah, that's what I said. That's when Furry started talking."

"Oh," I said. I glanced at the Marine. "So what'd you say? Anything smart?"

"Always," he said. "Look, I got dogs back home. They got this heightened sense of hearing, right? Stuff normal humans can't hear. I'm thinking Zulu operates the same way. I think if we hijack a tower on the west side of D.C. to emit a dog whistle and play it through the phones, they'll all go crazy trying to get it."

I let out a breath. "So, what happens when they wreck the tower?"

Furry hesitated. "Well—"

Sanchez cut in. "His genius idea was that we defend the tower as long as we can to keep the Zs occupied so the civilians can run to evac."

Silence fell.

Finally, Russell said. "Wow. They weren't kidding. You jarheads *are* crazy."

I settled back on my haunches. "To be clear, you guys think we should set up a giant zombie magnet in the middle of Washington Z.C. to attract every psycho cannibal in the area to *us*?"

I looked at Gunny. "How many would we even be looking at?"

Gunny whistled low. "Hundreds of thousands. Millions, if we include Baltimore, Arlington, Quantico…."

He trailed off.

Ferreira leaned forward, intense. "Look, once we get past a couple hundred, numbers don't exactly matter anymore, right? All we gotta do is hold that position for as long as humanly possible, sending out Dakota's weird little porno signal, then air evac out once we know we're losing. I mean, it's going to take Z some time to figure himself out once the signal dies, and that will at least let everybody on the east side of D.C. make it out to Kent before this Air Force guy's bombs drop."

"Hey," Russell said. "That's not *my* plan. They ain't *my* bombs."

"You know what you're asking, right?" Gunny said, looking at each of Alpha. "You guys don't have combat experience, not like the sergeant and I have. It's real unlikely we'll get evacuated out of a mess like that."

Dominguez fiddled with his rifle strap. "Yeah, but we were talking. We really liked helping the Garmins, Gunny. We *really* liked it."

He looked me in the eye. "We weren't running. We weren't sneaking. We were taking it to them, repelling Zulu by fire and close combat to save people who needed us. They *needed* us."

"Yeah," Sanchez said. "And Marine Corps history, our history, is full of Marines being outnumbered, doing what needed to be done. What, are we going to be the first ones to break that?"

I glanced at Gunny, who held something like tears in his eyes. "Every time," he said, "I think we're done, that America's done, I hear some of you kids talking and it restores my faith in the whole thing."

He looked over at me. "What do you think, Sergeant?"

I blew out my breath in a sigh. "It's a good plan. But we're talking millions of Zs running right for us. Even if we could rig the buildings to blow, we're not going to hold them for more than a couple seconds. They're going to rip that tower down in less than a minute and we're screwed anyway. Not sure that kind of return is worth our lives."

"It's worth *my* life," Dakota offered. "I'm not worth that much."

"Furry's not, either," Sanchez said. He glared at her.

"What? Wherever are we going to find another Boston Marine with a big nose and bigger mouth?"

"Probably the same place they keep finding loud Latinas with four baby daddies," Furry said, and yelped as she hit him.

"Aight," TSgt Russell interjected, "y'all convinced me. I'll go."

We looked at each other, then back at him. "Convinced you of what, TSgt?" Gunny asked.

"Now I realize," Russell said in his thick drawl, "that y'all Marines think being well-read is like a really deep color of crimson—"

"Yes," Dakota said immediately, and we chuckled.

"—but this plan of yours has the whiff of history to it. They'd be talking about the jarhead squad that evac'ed D.C. for fifty years after this, like Dunkirk or something."

"Your point?" I asked.

Russell put a hand on his chest. "So the Air Force wants a piece of this one."

"Hm," Dominguez said. "Another M4 in the fight. That's what, another .15 seconds of life?"

"Son," Russell said, giving him a sidelong look. He tapped the radio on his shoulder. "Do you know what this is?"

"PEZ dispenser," Dom said immediately.

"Sex hotline?" Furry offered.

"HQ, I need some AC! Stat!" Dakota pantomimed.

Russell looked at me. "This what it's always like with these kids?"

I gave him a tired smile. "You miss it when it's gone."

I sliced a hand at my band of retarded miscreants. "Enough. It's his radio."

"Ooo," Sanchez said in a caveman voice. "Does man of air make fire, too?"

They laughed until I said, "It's the radio of an Air Force combat controller, which makes it the most lethal weapon available to infantry."

That shut them up.

I pointed up. "Where do you think that F22 Raptor came from, geniuses? Tech Sergeant Russell here has access to Langley's fighter-bomber squadrons, if not the Navy squadrons sitting in the Bay."

The controller leaned forward. "So here's the deal," he said quietly, "take me with you. Set me up with some good visual observation of your target area and a real comfy chair, and I'll bomb your little zombie problem back to Hell."

"Ha!" Furry said. "He said chair."

Russell glanced at them. "Let's me kick back and watch while they eat you."

****

"So, here's where we get to some dubious legality," Dakota said.

Gunny grinned. "Wouldn't be a lance plan without some dubious legality, eh, Sergeant?"

I sighed. "Is this 'lose stripes' dubious legality or just a regular Article 15?"

Dakota put his hands on his hips. "Look, I got a buddy stationed in the FEMA tent, Lance Corporal Cavanaugh. We were in the same DEP, went to boot camp together and wound up in Twenty-Nine Palms for radio training at the same time. He can use the FEMA system to put out the signal we need."

I chewed on that. "Okaaaaaay. That's kinda dubious. Seems like wrist-slap stuff, though."

"Who gave us the Detrick mission, Sergeant?" Sanchez asked, spitting some dip juice into a bottle.

That hit me.

"Crap," I said, looking at Gunny.

"Why are you saying that? What don't I know?" Russell asked.

"We got our mission to Patient Zero in Ft. Detrick from the deputy director of FEMA, a guy named Whitney. He got his orders from Morano," I said. "That fat dweeb lives in that tent; it's where his power is."

"As soon as they find out what we're doing," Dakota slashed his hand across his throat, "they'll cut the signal and leave us to hang."

"I'm very unhappy right now," I muttered.

"So," Dakota went on, "and stop me if I sound like Nicholas Cage…"

"Ooo, ooo!" Furry said. "I wanna say it!"

I looked at them, not comprehending.

"Fine, you do it," Dakota said, irritated.

Furry put on a serious face. "I'm going to steal the Declaration of Independence."

"Still not getting it, guys," I said.

Russell started laughing. "Oh, man," he said, "y'all are too much. Our E3s don't pull this kind of shenanigans. They don't even *think* like this! Y'all are on a whole 'nother level."

He crouched down by Dakota and looked the kid in the eye. "Y'all wanna *kidnap* the deputy director of the Federal Emergency Management Agency. Amirite?"

My eyes widened and I looked at Dakota. "Tell me Air Force is wrong. Tell me he just disrespects my beloved Corps and that my lance corporals would never float that kind of treasonous theory where I could hear it and be forced to report it."

Sanchez shrugged. "It's not kidnapping, Sergeant. It's borrowing."

"For like an hour," Furry put in.

"He's basically the President!" I shouted.

Something howled somewhere, and Russell muttered, "Careful, man."

I dropped my voice. "He's basically the President until they find the next guy in the chain. How are you going to kidnap basically the President?"

Dominguez just grinned. "Sergeant Major hates him."

Gunny chuckled. The sound startled me. "They're right, Sergeant Major Hawke just needs to hear that his Marines are getting left high and dry. The problem will become solved."

I chewed on my lip. "So that's a sadge madge problem?"

Gunny shrugged. "Seems that way to me."

He turned back to what was left of my squad. "That is not our problem, though, is it, Dakota?"

Dakota looked glum.

I glared at him. "Ok, now what is it?"

He scritched at the fade on the back of his neck. "Look, I can take Cavanaugh's signal and tie into a tower to draw the Zs to us. We're basically going to create an ambulance effect where the signal continues propagating from phones and tablets all along the signal path to the tower we choose. That tower will become the source of the signal, the loudest thing around. It will be the difference between a crowd roaring at a concert and the guy on stage with the microphone."

"So what's the issue?" I asked.

"The problem is the interface gear. The software in the towers is proprietary, but there's secret squirrel stuff that SIGINT and NSA types get access to that can override it. I need that gear to make this work."

I glanced at Gunny. "SIGINT? That's 2nd Radio, right?"

Gunny shook his head. "We won't get them, not in time," he said. "Lejeune's got problems of its own."

I looked at Russell. "You're not carrying anything like that, right?"

He held up his hands. "Don't look at me. I just put calls out; I don't listen to 'em."

I sighed and turned away, but he went on.

"But...."

Russell ticked up a finger. "What about ChiComs?"

My eyebrow quirked. "What are you talking about?"

He tapped his chin. "Whole reason Command wants to bomb this area is loss of national secrets to foreign espionage. We're looking at Russkies, ChiComs, Israelis, all kinds of intel types that are probably just now starting to execute missions to steal vulnerable secrets."

Dakota nodded, starting to get excited. "Sergeant, if we find some of those guys and snag their gear, I can hook us up to a tower easy."

I held up a hand. "Hold up. You think we should ambush foreign SpecOps teams in the middle of several million Zulus? Seems like we're moving farther away from sanity here."

Russell shrugged. "Hey, y'all are the ones who want to make a bunch of noise. I'm just here to enable your terrible decision-making."

I rubbed my eyes. I was starting to feel sore from the past few days, sleeping in the field for a week then dealing with this crap. "Can we at least get a lift?"

****

Russell called in a bird from local Army. Apparently, he had dedicated transport for his mission, so it was no problem to get the combat controller 'and escort' moved from point A to point B.

Which happened to be the United States Capitol.

It took a while to decide where we were going. Trying to anticipate the movements of foreign espionage agents who might be trying to steal national secrets in the middle of the zombie apocalypse proved to be a matter of opinion.

Finally, Gunny chopped a hand through a shouting match between Ferreira and Sanchez. "All right, that's it!"

Ferreira snarled, "Look, you can't assume they don't know more than us! They're probably looking underground or some sh—"

Gunny thumped him on the back of the kevlar. "I said lock it up, Marine!"

He looked at each one of us.

"Lowest common denominator, right now! Where's the first place you would go? Don't think tactically, don't think anything special. Where would you go *first*?"

Each Marine said the same thing, and I had to reluctantly

agree.

The Potomac flashed beneath us, the sunlight sparking off of the water. The Blackhawk hung close to the surface, throwing up chop in the river. I sat in the door, my legs hanging over space as I surveyed the ruins of D.C.

I never liked the place. Too crowded, too full of altered history.

Didn't look any better now.

Crowds of Zs moved through the streets. They turned as one as our chopper blitzed past, their red eyes gleaming. I couldn't hear them over the thumping rotation of our bird's blades, but I saw them starting to run.

I tapped the side of my headset and opened a channel to Russell. "What's the touchdown plan?"

Russell stood on the other side of the chopper, one hand on his rifle as he hung on to the handle above him. His mic clicked in my ear. "Warrant officer here has been running transport missions all day. He says pilots have started buzzing the hordes to get them moving in a direction, then doubling back to drop off teams in the new quiet zones. Then the chopper buzzes the horde again to keep them moving in the wrong direction."

I squinted at him. "That work?"

He shrugged. "Most of the time. Sometimes, the team is stupid and starts taking shots. Turns the Zs around real quick."

I nodded. "Not stupid it is, then."

"That would be optimal, yeah."

****

So 'buzzing the horde' was exciting.

We were getting close to the Capitol. I could see the Smithsonian flash past, several memorials, the green grass of the Capitol lawn before everything swung around.

All we got from the pilot was a "Hang on, crayon eaters!" before the Blackhawk dropped like a stone. My heart jumped into my throat as we went weightless for a terrifying few seconds, before the chopper leveled out suddenly. The door gunners opened up with their chain guns as the Blackhawk slewed around, and I saw the massive crowd on the lawn and in the street. Sprays of black gouted into the air as the mini-guns played across the horde's flank.

"Got their attention," the pilot said, and then the chopper jerked forward, almost unseating me. Even though I was hooked in, I still grabbed for the handle next to me. Sanchez swore in terror, forgetting Gunny next to her, and Furry laughed uncontrollably as he slammed around from the bird's insane maneuvers.

"Independence Avenue, coming up in three zero," the pilot drawled, but I could still hear the tension in her voice. "Thank you for flying Air Army. Even in a world with no other options, using us was still a choice."

The bird banked left and buildings flashed past my vision. This was the double back.

"Get ready to go, Marines!" I shouted. Alpha sat up, unhooking seatbelts and grabbing gear.

A square building zipped under us. I caught sight of a sign: the Cannon House Office Building. The pilot was breaking line of sight to the horde, dropping us off, then racing back out to get them off us.

The chopper dropped, crunching into the pavement and jamming my spine. "I highly recommend you not wait for the aircraft to come to a complete stop!" the warrant shouted.

Didn't have to tell us twice. We spilled out from the chopper's sides, Dakota falling on his face in his zeal to get out. I didn't ding him for it. It was his first aerial insertion. We all did it at some point. TSgt Russell snagged the loop on his pack and jerked him to his feet.

I charged for the side of the Cannon House Office Building, letting the Marines see me and follow. Behind us, the chopper rocketed back into the sky, arcing around the side of the building and tearing off west. With the thunder of the bird's rotors out of our ears, now we could hear the Howl.

It was worse.

Before, we heard the sound of hundreds. That was bad enough. I'd had dozens screaming in my face back at Detrick. It's this awful gasping roar that sounds like a turbine sucking in air combined with a tiger growl.

That was nothing compared to Z.C.

We slammed into the side of the building, trying to reorient ourselves with the sheer wrongness of the ambient sound. A city should sound like cars, horns, shouting and the muted roar of people talking.

Not this time. Not here.

It was *thousands*.

It was like the Howl itself keened through the choked streets, tossing trash with its force. Cars were everywhere on the road, turned sideways, flipped over, windows shattered or cracked open like cans of sardines. Alarms sounded in the distance, and they would ring until batteries died or their speakers fried, because no one was coming to shut them off. The Howl echoed from the sides of the buildings, rebounding wildly so we couldn't tell where it came from.

My eyes darted everywhere as I ran forward in a crouch, tracking the movement of a scrap of newspaper, a plastic bag. I looked behind, and that's when I saw Ferreira's face. The kid was pale, his eyes wide. He was not okay.

I glanced at the others. It was the same. Gunny Hudson had a scowl on his face, as if he was trying to work out a problem.

I held up a fist before we crossed the threshold of the corner, and the squad melted into the side of the building. The road we were on, C Street SE, turned onto New Jersey Avenue, SE, which ran straight into Independence Avenue, the street running alongside the Capitol.

"What's up, Sergeant?" Gunny asked.

I glanced meaningfully at the younger enlisted.

"We got a minute, Marines," I said. "Take a breath. Adjust."

Furry nodded, taking deep breaths through his nose and out his mouth, and Dakota took a swig from his hydration system. Dominguez fingered a cross wrapped around his neck, muttering a prayer.

Unbidden, a faint smile touched my lips. "Hey."

They looked at me, pale and jittery.

"You guys wanted this."

Sanchez grunted in scorn. "Yeah, we keep signing up for stupid sh—crap. Was gonna say crap, Gunny."

"Sure, you were. See me COB for your counseling," Gunny muttered, and quick grins flashed all around.

I pointed a knife hand at them. "Same rules, Marines. I know it's weird. It sounds like Hell itself out there."

Dom nodded, still clutching that cross.

"But we're Marines, and Hell's where we regroup."

Furry nodded, some color coming back to his face. "Devil dogs," he muttered.

"Any of this for me?" Russell whispered, and I caught the look in his eye. He was trying to settle the younger enlisted, too.

"Why?" Sanchez asked. "You need a hug, Air Force?"

"I'm not saying no to some SAPI-on-SAPI action," Russell said, and I saw tension bleed out of my Marine's shoulders at the familiar back-and-forth.

"Aight, lock it up," I said. "Chopper probably dragged every Zulu after it that it could, which is a lot on this open ground in front of the Capitol. Keep low. We know their eyesight sucks, so keep quiet, too. Do not fire your weapons unless you absolutely have to. Careful when you open doors; one or forty of them might be stuck in there."

I looked each Marine in the eye. "We don't know what we're going to run into here. Might be nothing at all, might be every foreign intelligence asset on the East Coast. Stay frosty, and show them why we're the best."

Their hands gripped their weapons without shaking now. "Oorah, Sergeant," Sanchez said and the rest repeated after her.

I circled my hand for *assemble*, and six Marines and an airman moved out into overthrown D.C.

Chapter 16 - CAPITOL PUNISHMENT

We hugged the buildings as we moved north on New Jersey Avenue. I figured our cammies would break up our outlines more easily that way, and keep any Zs from accidentally seeing us. I saw Independence ahead, and beyond that, the bright white of the Capitol building.

Flags drooped forlornly from the buildings around us, and little American flag napkins blew along the deserted streets. A stark reminder that we were supposed to be celebrating the birth of our country.

Not its end.

For some reason, that pissed me off. My breath grew a little more ragged. I've always had a temper problem, especially when something unjust was happening around me. It had gotten me into trouble a lot as a kid, and even more as an adult.

I saw movement, and my rifle jerked toward it. It was just half a Z, snarling monotonously as it pulled itself along the street. Long ropes of gut trailed behind it, leaving a long blood stain on the asphalt. I held up a finger, signed the number three, and Dom broke out of line. He was the third Marine in line, and we had all decided he was going to be our quiet killer.

We kept our rifles up, covering him as he padded toward the struggling zombie. He slung his rifle behind his back and pulled his grandpa's Ka-Bar out. In one smooth maneuver, he launched himself into the air and slammed his knee into the thing's back, the half of it still there. His weight crushed any breath in its lungs before it could emit the Howl, his gloved hand jerked up on its jaw to clamp its mouth shut and expose its throat, and his blade rammed into the soft tissue there.

He did the usual trick we all learned in knife training. He twisted the knife and tore the blade across its throat, slicing through the windpipe and all the muscles. The problem was, he was still hauling back on the thing's head, and it was pretty ruined already.

All things added up to Dominguez's technique ripping the zombie's head clear off of its body with a disgusting squelch and a spray of black blood.

We all froze, and even Dom stumbled back, surprised at the result. He kept his wits about him and didn't drop the head. It gnashed at him with its broken teeth, its red eyes locked onto him as it growled silently. Still not dead. Unreal.

He gently set it down to bite at the concrete for however long it had left and padded over to us.

"What are you, the freaking Predator?" Furry whispered fiercely.

"I didn't mean to," Dominguez muttered.

"'I didn't mean to?'" Furry fired back. "That's what you say to your girlfriend after you sleep with her sister, not when you rip a zombie's head clean off its body!"

"Classy," Sanchez said, but she gave Dom a sidelong glance, too.

"Decomp," Gunny said quietly. "Keep that in mind. The longer these things walk around, the more their bodies are going to fall part. Try not to get any on you."

"You heard him. Zulu's getting squishy. Let's go," I said, and we moved off, leaving the headless half in the street.

****

Independence Avenue was deserted as we crossed. Looked like the Blackhawk had succeeded in drawing off pretty much all the Zs, and we were uncontested in our advance.

The devastation of the Capitol grounds spread out before us, and we were silent for more than one reason as we jogged through the ruins.

July 4 is a day of picnics and museum visits for most Americans. On Independence Day, the National Mall would have been packed with tourists, foreign and domestic, laying out blankets, sitting in lawn chairs with sunglasses and lemonades as salesmen hawked hot dogs and popsicles. Kites would have been flying, dogs running, kids playing.

"Sweet mother," Gunny whispered, and I had to agree with the sentiment.

The lawn in front of the Capitol was littered with a clown's checkerboard of broken chairs, ripped blankets and trash. Old blood spattered over everything, uniting the disparate riot of color with one unifying theme; dark brown. There were some bodies, torn apart beyond whatever this virus's ability was to reanimate.

Most of these were kids. Smaller, weaker; they had been ripped apart before they could turn. I could not imagine the carnage that took place here as the virus ripped its way through the packed crowds.

My Marines hesitated, and I heard a few gasps.

"Don't look, guys," I said, my jaw clenched til my teeth ground together. The darkness was coming back as I remembered those gas capsules back Detrick. I had to wonder if I'd find one on the ground somewhere if I looked hard enough.

Morano was going to pay for doing this to us. I swore it right then and there.

The next time I see you, witch, I'm going to rip your freaking head off your freaking pencil neck.

The four younger Marines stayed dead silent as we picked our way through the carnage. All I heard were Sanchez's quiet intakes of breath as tears tracked down her face.

"Sergeant," Russell said, and I looked at him. He pointed, and I saw it.

An AK-47 lay on the ground, a nice one. Fresh blood spattered across its grip.

I nodded. "Good catch, Air Force."

I looked around, looking for new clues now. "Eyes up, Marines. We got Russians."

****

7.62 casings lay scattered across the ground.

Russell kicked one over. "One of their team went down here. Probably drew the others to him."

I squinted and cocked my head. "Blood trail, too. He was wounded before he got here."

"Uh, Sergeant?" Dominguez asked.

I glanced at him. He was looking at a point along the blood trail. A wide spatter there, with a long squirt.

Russell whistled lowly. "That's a gunshot wound."

I grunted. "Yeah. Sounds like Russians to me."

"Wait," Dakota said. "His *team* shot him?"

Gunny crouched down and looked at us all. "Yeah. Shot him, left him for the other Zs to find so the rest of the team could get inside. Next time you wanna complain about the Marine Corps, suck it up."

That shut them up.

I drifted closer to Russell and Gunny. "KGB runs in teams of five," I said. "So there's probably four left in there."

"If they're still there," Russell pointed out.

"Blood's fresh," Gunny said. "Capitol's big, and they're unfamiliar with it. They're still there."

Gunny glanced at me. "Their teams have five, huh? You have some kinda experience with Russian teams?"

I sucked on a tooth. "Yeah. Once upon a time in Afghanistan."

He and Russell looked at me, waiting, but I wasn't doing story time. I didn't talk about that day. Lot of blood, lot of screaming. Guys stopped making fun of my surname after that.

It was also why I was a thirteen-year sergeant. I'd pissed off some Agency types over there, and every time I came up for promotion, something always jacked it up. Big Marine Corps didn't know what to do with me. They finally decided to ignore the whole incident and hope it didn't happen again, which suited me just fine.

Gunny didn't ask anything else, and I had a feeling he might know more about that day then he was letting on.

"Set up," I said quietly, "over there."

I pointed out the Washington Monument. It had an entrance to it; would make a good gun nest.

"And what will you be doing?" Gunny asked sharply.

I cracked my neck. "They probably have a sniper set up somewhere. Gotta flush him out."

Russell grunted. "I can do that."

I shook my head. "No, we need your radio and your authorizations for the hard part later on. I'm just a jarhead."

"Bullet magnet," Russell joked, but his brow furrowed in concern.

"Besides," I said, "Any sniper already set up is going to wait until he sees all of us. He's not going to waste a round on a lone Marine, knowing he'll give away his position."

Gunny peered at me intently, then said, "All right, then. We'll play it your way, Sergeant. Stay safe, stay in contact. No heroics, or whatever it is that you do."

I shrugged. "You know me."

"Oh, great," Ferreira said. "Now someone else gonna get their head ripped off."

****

I picked my way through the tangled debris of the Capitol picnic, rifle held at the ready position.

I'd lied.

Russians wouldn't have a sniper set up here, not for a smash-and-grab. In all honesty, I just didn't want the others with me for this.

The last time I'd tangled with Russians, a dark part of me had won out. I'd lost Marines that day, and I took that back in the enemy's blood. I wasn't willing for any of Alpha to be part of the death toll this time... or see me like that. I'd probably taken ten showers before I finally felt like I was clean again.

I set those memories aside and moved toward the side entrance of the Capitol, closest to Independence Avenue. Gunny had set Alpha up in the House Triangle about fifty yards off, not the monument like I said. As soon as gunfire cracked off, they would be ideally situated to repel with the SAWs operated by Furry and Sanchez.

Gunny was a good guy. I hope he knows how much I appreciated that.

The front of the Capitol was absolutely riddled with bullet holes. From the casings on the ground, these were 5.56, so American M4s and M16s. Blood everywhere, evidence of grenade use, chopper fire. This had been a warzone.

I hit my radio. "Air Force, you copy?"

"Marine Corps, this is Air Force. What can I do you for?"

I glanced around. "You know something about a military action here?"

A pause.

"Yeah, I heard something on the radio about the 101st Airborne trying to evac politicians once things went nuts. From what I could tell, it didn't go so great."

I blew my breath out slowly. "Yeah. Looks that way."

I skirted the front to the side. I didn't want to walk in the front door and surprise any armed foreign looters. For the same reason, I switched my radio to mute so Ferreira didn't accidentally get me killed.

Turns out, the armed foreign looters had the same idea, because I found their entry point. The side entrance of the Capitol had been breached. A metal door lay to the side, the edges ragged from the powered saw discarded nearby. Several Zs lay on the ground, holes in the backs of their heads.

I moved inside, my rifle sweeping the corridor as I moved from light into semi-darkness. Broken furniture, cloth guard rails, portraits and flags littered the floor. Security barricades lay on their sides, and I saw several discarded weapons on the floor.

Again, bullet holes and blood everywhere. This had been a serious battle. I wondered how well the 101st came off.

I passed by tall portraits of presidents, long rips in the lower half of the canvas. Splintered podiums, scattered paperwork, a severed arm: these greeted me as I moved down the hallway of our nation's seat of governance.

I could hear someone ahead of me. Sounded like they were looting the offices.

Made sense. Our politicians weren't exactly known for treating classified documents with the security they required. Easy pickings for an espionage team.

I hesitated before moving up the stairs. I was probably about to see people I watched on TV, this time with bites or holes in them.

Heh. Politicians eaten by the people. That would be hilarious.

I stepped slowly up the stairs, setting each heel down carefully to prevent unnecessary sound. These Russkies were probably expecting Zulu interference, not a Marine going stealth mode, so their radar wouldn't be too far up.

I heard movement from a nearby office. *And Bingo was his name-o.*

Sure enough, I edged around the corner and saw my first one. Big blonde guy, hair cut like Guile from Street Fighter. He wore coveralls with a black molly-webbed vest, AK-74 on the table next to him.

Odd choice, that weapon. Used a different round than the 47 did, the 5.45. Didn't like to share ammo; not a team player, then.

Good. No one will care when you die.

I crept up on him, glancing both ways to ensure he was alone. I knew the team would likely scatter to cover the most ground once they breached the Capitol and secured it. The KGB agent was focused sifting through a stack of papers, no doubt trying to put his limited English reading skills to use.

He didn't notice me until I looped an arm under his chin,

cinched my lock and fell backwards. My legs clamped around his hips like a boa, and I rolled my shoulders back, locking in my blood choke with all the practice I'd put in at the dojo. My bicep and forearm pinched the arteries in his neck shut.

Boris fought it good. He lasted about eight seconds before his eyes rolled back, but he wasn't getting out of a Marine's blood choke, especially one as big as me.

Sure enough, my little Russkie quit flopping and relaxed. I kept the hold for a few more seconds to make sure he wasn't faking, then eased him down.

Time to find the rest of them—

His radio squawked. *"Mikhail, zdes' nichego net. Gruppa na nas."*

I closed my eyes, cursing fate and God and whatever else. *Fifteen seconds later, he could have answered that and I would be golden.*

There was no use picking up the radio. I didn't speak Russian, and they were gonna know that.

"Mikhail."

I reached for my radio as I clicked my selector off safe. "Gunny, you're going to hear some noise. Stay put."

I heard footsteps pounding down the hall and my sight hardened to a glare. "I'm fine."

Chapter 17 - IVAN

Ten minutes later, I growled more than breathed. The wind pulsed in and out of my chest in great gusts as I moved into the atrium, cheek to my stock and eye to my RCO. I could feel the blood drying on my face.

"Sergeant," my radio squawked. Gunny again.

I had no time for him. I was in kill mode, and I could sense more of the enemy nearby. This was my pure state, my blood chilled yet boiling in my veins at the same time. My fingers wrapped around my rifle with brutal intensity, and I felt like the metal should be warping under my fury.

My eyes flicked from high point to high point, searching for threats. I'd killed three of them so far. The gunfire had attracted a crowd of Zs from a nearby set of offices, and it had taken me a couple of minutes to drop them all.

"Sergeant," Gunny insisted.

My lips twisted, but I tapped the PTT on my shoulder. "This is Slaughter. Go."

"You're making a lot of noise in there and we've got movement outside, moving to your location. Hold so the squad can back you up."

"Hang on," I snarled. "I don't need you yet."

"I don't think you heard me properly, Sergeant," came the response. *"Get out of the Capitol. Now."*

Blood and guts decorated my cammies. I'd blown through that last crowd of Zs like a Mack truck. The more I killed, the less I feared them.

There was nothing here that concerned me, and I opened my mouth to tell him that.

All of that was before I saw it. My hand froze on the mic trigger as I stared at the single item telling me my life was pretty much over.

Wasn't a nuke. Wasn't a bomb. Wasn't a bioweapon, or a super-zombie, or anything like that.

Nope.

It was a hammer.

A simple sledgehammer stood on its head on a pedestal in the atrium, out of place amidst the devastation. It had been placed there. Recently.

And I knew who had done it.

My kill state elevated to a point I had experienced only once before, as the sheer threat of the situation magnified to apocalyptic levels. I stalked the streets of America's once-greatest city, swarming with mobs of the undead, and yet here was the sign of an even greater threat, something elemental in its primal savagery.

"We're coming in. Hold your fire," Gunny growled.

I snatched my radio so fast, I thought I broke it. "Belay that, Gunny," I said. "Do not enter, I repeat, do not enter."

"Sergeant?" Gunny responded. *"I don't have time for your Lone Ranger Rambo crusade—"*

I heard the edge in his voice. He thought I was losing it. That was all right. I knew I was losing it.

This wasn't that, though. So I cut him off.

"Gunny, you send Alpha in here, they'll just get killed," I whispered harshly, circling slowly. "Pull them back, hunker down. I'll let you know when it's safe."

"Marine," Hudson snarled, *"You will fall back to our position and we will tackle this as brothers—"*

"Gunny," I snarled, and the radio fell silent. "It's an Ivan."

A pause.

"I don't know what that means."

"Yeah, but I do. Listen to me and stay out."

I panned my weapon around the room, struggling to summarize this enough for him in the little time I had left to live.

"I found out about Crazy Ivans in Afghanistan a few years back. They were drugged and trained by the Soviets to be indoctrinated super-soldiers in the Cold War. High fatality rates, mostly since they couldn't be controlled and went insane from the drug use. Whatever target they were sent after died. They were like suicide soldiers, but instead of wearing the bombs, they *were* the bombs."

"Only one lived to be old, and I'm looking at his calling card right now."

"Hold up. You know him?" Gunny asked.

I glanced at the hammer on the floor. "Met him once, on a really, really bad day. Keep my Marines out of here, Gunny. I'm not kidding you."

After a moment, the radio came back. *"Heard. I'm trusting you, Slaughter."*

I cracked my neck and moved in.

****

"I know you're here," I said.

In the silence of the atrium, I knew he could hear me. "Come out. I know hiding isn't your thing, and if you wanted me dead, I'd already be on the floor."

The atrium itself was one of those large open rooms with the double curved staircases going to the second floor. The walls and ceilings were white, where they weren't streaked with blood. Hardwood trim everywhere, papers scattered across the floor, some loose brass. Half the room was lit by the sunlight streaming through the windows in the roof. The rest was cast in deep shadow.

A door cracked open behind me. That was not a mistake, not by this killer. He was just being polite by giving me an indicator of his location. Professional.

I turned slowly, lowering the barrel of my rifle as I did, though keeping it in the ready position.

Ivan emerged from a side room. The tip of his filthy cigar glowed orange in the near-darkness, illuminating his gray beard and lined face. His unblinking eyes gleamed with that crazy ice-blue, like a husky's.

The man was huge. Soviets weren't known for their

restraint when it came to using steroids, and again, I marveled at the sheer violence the man exuded. His chest rose and fell like a bellows. Hair sprouted all over his thick arms, and the reek of vodka washed over me, banishing for a second the ever-present rot.

He held an AK-47 in his hands, grenades strapped along his belt, bandoliers of rounds across his chest. If he wasn't so lethal, he would have been cartoonish.

"Where's the scythe?" I asked, sliding back a step. Distance was good.

He stepped forward into the light, a slow grin spreading across his face. "Could not bring," he answered, accent as thick as the rest of him. The man had only learned English so he could understand what his victims babbled as they died. He knew lots of languages. "And hardware store carries wrong kind."

I blew my breath out slowly as he approached. The man was a monster in every sense of the word, and my life hung by the fraying thread of his sanity.

As he passed it, Ivan reached out and lifted the hammer from its place. He whirled it once, letting the weight of the hammer head sling it around, before slicing it before him in a figure eight.

"Interesting times we live in, eh, *chort*?" he asked, a grin splitting his weathered face.

I'd actually had to look that term up after our last encounter. He was calling me 'demon' in Russian.

"I confess, I was not sure if you would live through *voskresshie* rising. I should have known better. There is no killing a killer when Death rules."

I cracked my neck. "What are you doing here, man? Afghanistan get you scared?"

Ivan grunted in derision. "Ha! The graveyard of empires has no hold on me. I get bored."

"So, you're just in D.C., seeing the sights?" I sidestepped in a circle, the barrel of my weapon lowered, but ready to whip it up.

Ivan grinned at me. "There is so much to see now. You see, in motherland, we say capitalists eat each other. I did not think to take literally until two days ago."

He spread his arms wide, taking in the ruined atrium. "No, I came here to see faded glory of empire that felled my beloved *Sojuz Sovetskich Socialisticeskich Respublik.* To breathe the air of the capitalist pigs who declare themselves better than the Boss."

Ivan stepped closer, looming over me. "To see country that made *you.*"

My turn to grunt. "Gotta head west for that. Texas is nothing like D.C., trust me."

His bushy brow furrowed. "You are... cowboy?"

I smiled wryly, thinking of TSgt Russell. "Not every Texan's a cowboy, but yeah. I worked my uncle's ranch."

He tapped his chest. "My uncle, also, was shepherd. His flocks were taken by party for good of all."

"I'm sure he loved that," I said, stepping in a wide circle away from him.

Ivan shrugged, metal teeth gleaming in his grin. "He tried to fight. Was shame to kill him in front of family."

"Sounds rough at holidays," I said.

"Sergeant, incoming." Gunny sounded tense.

The Howl rose beyond the walls of the Capitol, broken doors banging and furniture turning over. I sighed and hit my radio. "Heard, Gunny. Still good in here."

I turned back to Ivan.

"Round two is heading our way," I said, lifting my rifle. "Resume after?"

The big Russian commando slung his hammer over his back and hefted his AK. "Of course. Will be privilege to see *chort* kill again."

I sighed. "Don't call me that."

****

They poured toward us down the hallways like a river of diseased flesh, hundreds of Zs clawing to get past each other. Ivan and I stood back-to-back in the atrium of the Capitol, my M4 tucked into my shoulder, Ivan holding his AK low at the hip.

As soon as the horde tightened up to burst through the narrow doorway, I fired. A Z's head snapped back with a spray of black.

I did not switch to burst mode. I don't even know why the selector switch on the M4 goes to three-round burst, unless it's to burn through ammo so we can go home early on a range day. But I did rapid-fire squeeze the trigger, panning the weapon across the necklines of the horde. Bodies hit the floor, gore spilling out from popped skulls.

At my back, something exploded, rocking me forward, and bits of meat and bone sprayed past me as the pressure wave gripped my lungs. The bass chatter of Ivan's AK mixed with his hoarse growl that passed for laughter.

Ivan loved his bombs. I had shrapnel scars in my legs to remind me of that.

Corpses, the unmoving kind, stacked up in my doorway, blocking their buddies' ingress. The Zs, hunger desperate in their crimson eyes, shrieked and reached for me. Precise as surgery, the barrel of my M4 twitched over, sighting for an instant before I pulled the trigger. Zombies crashed to the floor or sagged, held upright by their buddies piling in.

As soon as they hit critical mass, I shouted, "Switch!"

I spun around as Ivan underhanded a live grenade into my doorway. The explosive arced over the heads of the undead swarm; its placement perfect. One thing I had to give this psycho freak... he knew his kabooms.

The resulting detonation shook the atrium, but my stack in the doorway didn't even tip over. As a matter of fact, even more shredded zombies slumped against it, sealing the entryway shut. The man was unreal in his precision.

But on his side, zombies spilled through, and I rushed forward to meet them.

The butt of my rifle crunched through a rotten temple, snapping the bone. I whipped it back around, swiping away the blackened hands reaching for my neck, and emptied my magazine point-blank into the mob.

Most of the Zs were dressed in civilian attire, picnickers for the July 4 on Capitol grounds. Some were in guard attire. And some were in Army fatigues, 101st patches on their arms.

Guess it really didn't go great for them.

I saw all of this in a second, and then my rifle ran dry.

"Ivan!" I shouted. "Gotta go!"

His AK wasn't barking anymore, either, and neither one of us could take the three seconds to swap out mags.

The burly Russian roared and backhanded his sledge hammer in a brutal lateral swing. Skulls popped like grapes as blood exploded from anything he hit. Ivan waded into the undead, his hammer whipping around him in looping arcs. Bodies flew from his crushing strikes.

My mind raced. We needed a point to hold. All the Zs in earshot were probably already here. We just needed a place, preferably high up, to—

I had an idea.

"Russkie!" I yelled. He twisted toward me, his beard clotted with gore. His eyes shone fiercely through the sticky mask of blood.

Yeah, that's about what I remember.

"Follow!"

****

We burst out of the Capitol building onto the wide stairway, Zs spilling out behind us. I had the mag well of my M4 in some dead woman's teeth, ramming her backwards as I bulled forward. Her jaws tried to chomp through, but her yellowed teeth chipped off on the gun metal.

I shoved her with all two hundred-seventy pounds, and she rocketed backward down the stairs. Her skull smacked into a corner of the concrete steps, and she stopped moving.

Below us, Zs clambered up the stairs. Behind us, they poured out of the Capitol building. But we had good line of sight now, and they were slow.

Our mags clicked into our weapons at the same time. I heard Ivan take another draw on that disgusting cigar in his mouth. I exhaled in a snarl, raised my rifle and started snapping off shots.

I took high, dropping the Zulus coming at us from the Capitol. Ivan held his AK-47 one-handed and sprayed the masses crawling toward us from the stairs. With the other, he stabbed his hammer into a Z's face, crushing its cheeks into its skull.

"Sergeant!" came the call from my radio.

I gunned down another two runners with a trio of shots before mashing the button on the radio to open mic. "Busy, Gunny!" I roared.

"I can see that," Hudson bit off. *"We have line of sight on you. We're going to push into the aft quadrant of the horde. We're coming from* your *left. Do not shoot us."*

I snarled in frustration, but I knew where he was coming from. Marines can't not join in a fight. Besides, he had better situational awareness of the field than I did and knew the risk he took.

"Ivan!" I shouted. "If you have grenades, chuck 'em now. Friendlies coming in from your left downstairs."

"What is this 'chuck 'em'?" Ivan called back through grit teeth. I didn't know why he even wanted to keep that cigar in his teeth. He was basically breathing Zulu blood at this point. All the heroin in his system must have been keeping him from turning.

"Throw them!" I yelled.

"Ah! I like this word!" he exclaimed. He slung his AK, took hold of the bandolier of grenades on his chest, and stripped off the pins with one swipe. He hefted the package once, letting the explosives cook.

"I chuck them now!"

But he didn't throw them into the horde down the stairs. No, that would have made tactical sense.

Instead, I should have remembered that Ivan was here to kill for pleasure and make memories, like an American-killing safari.

So, when the Russian turned and lobbed the bandolier of primed grenades directly into the Capitol building, through the wide doors we had come out of, I had no one to blame but myself.

I heard his mad laugh bark once before the explosives went off.

Ivan's grenades are custom. The bandolier clearly had something stronger in it than the usual frags, because what seemed like the entire front of the Capitol of the United States blew apart. The shockwave staggered me forward and I misstepped, stumbling down the stairs.

Straight into the untouched horde of Zs.

****

Hands clamped around my neck and mouth, pawing at my cammies, trying to drag me down. The Howl deafened me, and Zs screamed in my ear as they tried to get their teeth into me.

I bucked, throwing smaller Zs back. I lashed out with my fists, cracking jaws and bruising my knuckles. My breath sawed in and out of my lungs as panic laid heavy oxygen debt on my system.

A Z launched itself onto top of me, shrieking from a few steps up. I rode the impact, grabbed its arm and sledgehammered it into the concrete, knocking three more back.

In a flash, I pulled my M9 and emptied the magazine, strafing the bucking pistol across the surface of the horde at head level.

I set my heel back and felt the lip of the stair. Now I had my bearings and a second to breathe.

That was when I made a decision. Knowing what I know today has taught me it was a *terrible* decision.

You see, ordinarily, I would recommend against engaging the undead in hand-to-hand. In the months and years since that day, I've seen guys turn into mindless freaks from a bite, a scratch or even just getting some zombie splatter in their mouths. You absolutely should get as much distance between you and the biters, ideally with some height, and reach out and touch them with a comfortable safety buffer.

Not me. Not that day.

I elected hand-to-hand, and thank God He loves Marines.

My idiot self dropped my empty M9 into my dump pouch, got my rifle up just as the dead surged, and jumped into them.

I punched the stock forward, breaking teeth off in some undead chick's screaming face and wrecking the nose job that was already starting to slant.

A lot of these Zs were gonna look real weird when the meat decayed and the plastic didn't.

I followed up with a slash of the barrel, tearing some dead tourist's face sideways. Hands pawed at my back and I ducked enough to slip the bloody grips. I grabbed the Z above me by the belt and sidearmed him bodily into the crowd, staggering them back and clearing some space for my primary weapon.

Fire spit from my M4 as I snapped from target to target. Zulus tumbled down the concrete stairs, even as their buddies tripped on debris blown out by Ivan's bomb.

I could hear the Russian bellowing nearby, shouting in his mother tongue at the Zs swarming us. I could hear the squishing crunch of his hammer going to work.

At last, I heard the sweet, sweet sound of fuzzy bunnies flying from the barrels of two SAWs belonging to dedicated Marines.

I backed up another step and saw Alpha Squad walking

line abreast, their weapons kicking against their shoulders. Zombies hit the deck, brains blasting out of their filthy skulls as the Marines chewed through the backend of the mob like weed-whackers through brush.

It took about thirty seconds to thresh the mob down to nothing but twitching scraps.

I let out a big breath as Hudson walked up to me, checking the bodies at his feet for live ones.

"Sergeant," he said.

"Gunny," I answered. "Thanks for the assist."

"It's called back-up," he said pointedly, and I ducked my head.

"Uh, Sergeant?" Dakota said, staring at the flaming ruin behind me. "I don't know if you know this, but... ya blew up the *Capitol*."

The sudden letdown as the adrenaline fled my system threatened to put me on my knees. "Nah," I said, waving it off. "We'll just blame Russian interference on that one. Works every time."

Chapter 18 - BARELY LEGAL

"So," our neighborhood Russian psycho said. "These are fellow *chorti*?"

I nodded. "Alpha Squad, Ivan. Ivan, Alpha Squad."

"Sup," Dominguez said, giving the big Russian a once over.

"Did he just call me Shorty?" Sanchez asked. Her eyes glinted dangerously.

"Jeez, Sanchez," Ferreira said. "You're Mexican. You're short. I'd say get over it, but I know it's harder for you... cuz you're short."

As the lances lit into each other, TSgt Russell approached me.

"Thought you said he was dangerous," he said.

"He just blew up the Capitol of the United States," I said, wincing as the words left my lips. This after-action report was going to *suck*.

Ivan could not stop grinning. His teeth had to have dried out by now.

"It's every Soviet's wet dream," I continued. "After that high, I don't think he cares about killing Marines."

"Hm," the controller grunted. He planted his hands on his hips. "Welp, I called in an air strike to draw most Zs away, so I figure we got about fifteen minutes. He got what we need?"

I sighed. "Haven't had a chance to ask."

Ivan glanced at me. "What? What is it you wish to ask?"

I cracked my neck. "Well, before I knew it was *you*, I wanted to intercept a foreign espionage team I knew would be trying to take advantage of the—," I gestured at the ruin around, "—situation."

Ivan cocked his head. "What for?" he asked bluntly. "Marines are killers. You should be killing these *voskresshie,* not hunting spies."

I had to remind myself that just because Ivan was crazy,

that didn't mean he was dumb. There was a reason this warrior was still alive when every one of his compatriots had died.

Dakota stirred as if to speak, but I held up a hand. I really did not want my Marines talking to Ivan if I could help it.

"We need your comms gear," I said. "We figure you advanced teams have something we can use."

Ivan smiled amiably. "Sure," he said. "Young ones on team had pretty computers and antennas with them."

"Not you, though, huh?" I asked.

He shook his head, his teeth shining white beneath the black blood coating his face. "Too much faith in machines," he said. "Not enough in hammer and gun. Is why Chinese fell so quickly."

Ferreira grunted. "Heh, can't hack a zombie," he said. "Checkmate, fools!"

I looked back at Ivan. "I need that gear."

"What do I get for it?"

"Nothing. You're not using it."

"Is Soviet property."

"Soviets haven't been a thing in twenty-five years, Ivan."

"Has sentimental value."

"You don't feel things."

He peered at me. "You want so bad, eh? Fine. Will trade. Give—," he pretended to think for a moment, "—all secrets left in Capitol building."

He grinned at me, clearly waiting for my retort.

"Done," I said.

He kept smiling. "Sure, sure."

I didn't move. I just stared at him, waiting, until Ivan's grin started to fade.

"Sergeant," Gunny said, his tone warning.

"It's fine, Gunny," I said. "What are we losing?"

That wiped the smirk off the Russian's face. He looked from Gunny to me. "What? You are serious?"

He searched my face with his cold husky eyes, but I just didn't care. "The world's over, Ivan," I said quietly. "Look around. What's happening here is everywhere. You want national security secrets? Go take 'em. They don't matter anymore. If anything, they're about two days out of date."

Ivan hesitated.

I spread my hands out. "What do you want, Ivan? Dirt on politicians? Half of them are zombie jerky right now. How about procurement contracts for all those weapons no one's alive to build or use? Or nuke codes? You want *nuke codes*?"

I gestured at the ruined Capitol lawn, with hundreds of bodies spilled all over it. "Look at us, man. There's probably not enough of us left to even *bother* nuking."

I stabbed a finger in his face. "And if we look like this, the most powerful military in the entire world, what do you think is happening in Moscow? Huh? What do you think, Ivan?"

Ivan looked from me to the rest of Alpha, the shadows around his eyes deepening. He fingered his radio absently, and I realized he probably hadn't used the thing in days. "Is happening in Russia?" he asked finally.

I chuckled darkly. "What, you didn't ask why they stopped reaching out on comms?"

Ivan shrugged, looking sheepish. "I figured they finally leave me alone."

I breathed a sigh. I was so tired. "Go *home*, dude. You love your country; I know you do. Go take care of it. Go do what you do best, for what they need you to do."

He seemed strangely conflicted. I had no idea the level of psycho-indoctrination they had done to him, and abandoning orders had to be painful. I stepped forward and put a hand to his shoulder, and he blinked at the sudden contact. He probably couldn't remember the last time someone had touched him of their own volition.

"Most people," I said, "just want to build houses, go to school, and work their jobs. They aren't killers, not like us. They can't do what we do, and we sure can't do what they do. They need us, now more than ever."

He fingered his hammer for a bit, looking down at the

ground. It was fairly surreal to see this Russian engine of war shift his feet like a kid with butterflies in his stomach, but eventually Ivan nodded.

"I believe the word of the *chort*," he said firmly. "Mother Russia is in danger. I must go home to her."

He chucked a thumb behind him. "Check big blonde's gear. He scavenge Chinese equipment after I kill them. He will have."

Now it was Gunny's turn to blink. "Really? Just like that?"

Ivan looked down at him. "Marines do not lie," he said.

Russell's eyebrows went up, and he glanced at me. "That a fact?"

"Marines," Ivan repeated, his tone dead, "do not lie. I go."

He pointed at me and gestured between us with his finger. "This is not over, *chort*. We will learn who is better someday. Once homelands are safe, I will come, and I will kill."

With that, he strode past us.

"Can't wait. Be safe, Ivan," I muttered after him, and his laugh faded with him, disappearing into the desolation of D.C.

****

"Hey, Sergeant, is Mr. Coo-coo for Communism going to be, you know, okay?" Ferreira asked. We stood guard over Dakota as he picked through the Russian and Chinese gear.

I glanced at him. "Who, Ivan? You *worried* about him?"

"Well, like, a little, you know. He did help back there."

I stared. "He blew up the *Capitol*, Furry. Not sure I'd call that help. Besides, Ivan's a fire-and-forget. Russians aren't sentimental, and if anything, I think they're surprised he keeps coming back from whatever insane missions they send him on."

"I don't know, man," Ferreira said, rubbing the stubble on his jaw. "Like, does being Russian matter anymore? Like you were saying, in this world, would that guy even be a threat?"

I chuckled and let my head drop back. "Yeah, Furry. Ivan

will be a threat. Ivan will always be a threat. We got lucky today."

"So," Sanchez said, resting her hands on her slung 249, "what was that stuff he was talking about? Back in Afghanistan? He acted like he knew you. And he keeps calling you 'demon' in Russian."

"Yeah," Dominguez said. "And that 'Marines don't lie' stuff. Where's that come from?"

I exhaled quietly. I really didn't want to answer this question. "Old blood, from another time," I said, and left it at that.

Ferreira was stupid enough to try to get more out of me, but then Dakota stood up. "Got it," he said proudly, holding up a little black box.

"Great," said Dominguez. "What's that?"

"This," Dakota tapped the device, "is a secret squirrel box that can only be worked by secret squirrels and only talked about with said named squirrels."

He looked at us. "Any of you numbnuts squirrels?"

Gunny held up a hand. "We got it. You tell us, then you'd look real stupid trying to kill us. Can you use it?"

Dakota nodded, stuffing the box in his pack with a bunch of connectors and wires. "Yes, Gunny. I can."

He pointed at Ferreira and Dominguez. "So, keep me alive. I'm important now."

"Wow," Dom said. "Never seen so little power go to someone's head before."

"The infamous one-inch erection," Furry said, spitting a stream of dip spit to the side. I almost said something, as we were in the Capitol, but decided against it. I'd just let the front half get blown off. It was probably a little hypocritical to stand on decorum now.

"Come find me in the porta-john later, hotshot," Sanchez said, batting her eyes.

"Anyway," Dakota said, turning to me and Gunny and ignoring the others grandly, "now we just gotta get me to our broadcast point. I'll coordinate with Cavanaugh on the way."

"How you gonna do that?" Gunny asked, arching an eyebrow. "Morano's still monitoring our comms."

Dakota lifted a Russian radio and waggled it. "Not theeeeese."

****

The intricacies of each MOS in the Marine Corps is hard to explain.

We get assigned primary MOSs, like 03 for infantry, 18 for tankers, etc. Then we get other numbers that further break us down, like 0311 rifleman, 0331 machine gunner, 0341 mortar man, yada yada.

But all that's just in the computer system. Each MOS has its own family culture to it in the Marine Corps, which is already its own subculture in the military. Seriously, you should see how the other branches look at us when we're around. Army gets all stiff and challenged by us, and Navy is more curious than anything else. Air Force usually tries to call the cops on us.

Sometimes, that MOS subculture gets further defined by the shop you're in. We PT together, train together, eat together, drink together, take leave together and get divorced together. We're tightknit families where loyalty is everything and snitches get stitches. Woe be to the inexperienced lieutenant who tries to penetrate the Lance Corporal Underground and get any E3 or lower to rat on a fellow Marine.

Like the S1, our admin. office. Those Marines are all legally required to be dicks, and they are, on the rare days they're present in the office, with the single exception of that one super Marine in the shop who does an entire battalion's worth of paperwork by himself so that his Marines get taken care of. That kid never stands duty and never buys his own snacks. We take care of that brother *as a unit.*

Armory Marines are their own thing. Intel Marines are the same. God help you if you cross the range Marines; they'll have you brass-calling bare dirt 'til twenty-three hundred on a Friday. As a sergeant, sometimes I feel like an Hindu priest, trying to placate nineteen separate pagan gods in a day to get anything done.

The S6 shop is another one of these beasts. The S6 is our information and communications shop, but it behaves like the frigging Mafia. Every S6 door is full-on metal, always locked, and you can't see inside through the window. You poke your head in, ask a lance corporal with a haircut on the edge of regulation for something, and a few minutes later, having worked some dark sorcery, he gets your access issue gets resolved.

If the family likes you.

Dakota, being comms himself, had ties to the S6 crime family, though he was assigned to an infantry unit. Turns out, one of his little squirrel bastard friends had a hobby radio he kept on him, that he had managed to *design an app for* on his smartphone. The genius of lance corporals in my beloved Corps would never cease to amaze me.

"And you already talked to him?" I asked, hands on my hips as we took our hourly break.

Dakota swallowed a mouthful of granola and nodded. "Yeah, Cavanaugh's on board. He really, really hates that Whitney guy. He's already programmed the signal into the system and designed a pathway for the signal to propagate through the city."

I glanced at Gunny. "We are going to Super Jail after this. They'll reopen Guantanamo just for us."

Gunny just grinned. "Better make it work then, Sergeant, or we won't have any good stories to tell while we're breaking rocks into littler rocks. All right, Marines, sock-changing time. Let's go. Skivvy rolls out."

With the normal amount of grousing about Mother Guns, combat boots were unlaced, pulled off and set to the side while the brown disgusting socks on our feet were peeled off. After three days of this, the reek was something else.

"Whew," Ferreira called out. "We gotta bottle that and make some cheese or something."

"Yeah, or tequila," Sanchez said, pulling a skivvy roll out of her pack.

A skivvy roll, for the non-military reader, is a complete set of undergarments in a single self-contained roll. Basically, you lay out your skivvy shirt and PT shorts (also called skivvies for some reason), and lay a pair of socks across the chest of the shirt, the feet of the socks lying across each other while the holes face out. Then you roll the whole thing up from the bottom to make a tube, pull the holes of the socks over the shirt roll and bam — skivvy roll. Great for chucking at fellow Marines across a tent.

You can make cammy rolls, too, as long as you have boot bands. There's no better way to maximize space in your pack when you need a week of uniforms for a field exercise, or FEX.

Since we were on a FEX when this whole thing started, each of my Marines had several skivvy rolls in their packs. After several days of extended combat against Zulu and associates, not to mention hiking all of Maryland in combat boots, Gunny Hudson knew it was a good time to swap out socks and prevent foot rot.

"Make sure your feet are dry," Gunny reminded us. "If you got a sore, let me know and I'll drop by. I got some cream and moleskin."

Moleskin. It's the stuff they make Band-Aids out of. Does wonders for blisters and sores when you gotta keep hiking.

"Yeah, Gunny, let me have some," Dominguez said, and the man stepped over to him.

While Gunny helped Dom out, I leaned over to Dak. "So, is there a timeline we need to follow for this crazy plan of yours?"

Dakota sighed. "Cavanaugh said that the colonel's been in

contact with the Marine battalion on those Navy ships. They're dug into Kent Island, just like you thought, but people can't make the trip over the bridges because of all the Zs, and Whitney doesn't want Marines making expeditions out to get people because they're supposed to be protecting *him*."

I rubbed my mouth. "So, he's wanting to get out of there?"

Dakota nodded. "And the admiral is getting real tired of having to listen to him. He basically told Whitney if he couldn't get civilians on his ships, he'd leave Whitney, too."

I grinned. I love the Navy. Captains on their own ships are basically gods, and their chiefs think that they're the gods' toes, squishing everyone else. It was nice to see it working in our favor for once.

Something struck me and I lowered my voice. "He say anything about Morano being there?"

Dakota shook his head. "Said she lit out right after Detrick. Left Whitney high and dry, which pissed *him* off no end."

I nodded. "Well, maybe that's good. Let her be someone else's problem, then. Maybe she finally forgot about us."

Dakota squinted. "I don't know, Sergeant. She seems pretty anal about details. And we're the details."

Furry leaned in. "Actually, I'm the anal."

Sanchez blew her breath out rudely, but couldn't hide her sudden grin.

Chapter 19 - SHADOWS

The distance from the Capitol to our broadcast point in western D.C. was way shorter than I thought it would be. After talking with Gunny Hudson and TSgt Russell, we'd come to the conclusion that the best place for us to try to hold out was Ronald Reagan Washington National Airport.

Five miles down the road.

"Look," Russell said, pinching open the map on his phone. "The whole east side connects to the Cemetery by those bridges, which are the Theodore Roosevelt on the 66, the Memorial Bridge, the 14th Street Bridge and the 395. They have to funnel down from the north and then go through this massive open space before they could even reach us there. It's a heckuva kill zone, if I do say so myself."

Gunny nodded. "And the airport will have somewhere Dakota can hook up and set up that signal."

"Not to mention a helipad for evac after a successful mission," Russell said with a grin.

"Look at Air Force here," I said. "Wanting to live through a mission."

He slapped me on the shoulder. "Yeah, I know, man, we're soft."

We were talking about this on a break before crossing the bridge on the 66. I'd pointed out to Gunny that this was the long way, that the 395 was way shorter, but he waved me off.

"The Marines need to see something," was all he said.

"Aight," Gunny said, checking his watch. "Let's go. Marines, get 'em up. Light's fading. We're moving."

With groans, Alpha rousted itself up, settling packs back into place and reslinging weapons,

"Are we there yet?" Ferreira asked plaintively.

"Let's keep it locked up while we cross this bridge," I said, "No jokes, no unnecessary chatter. While we're on it, we're easy to pin, so let's stay frosty."

Nods, mutters and "heard" came back at me. I looked up. Gunny wasn't kidding, the sun was starting to set.

"Let's get across this bridge and find a place to set up for the night."

****

The seven of us moved along the bridge, hugging the right edge, silent as death. The bridge itself was packed with vehicles. Traffic in D.C. sucked even when its people had been alive; it had not improved in its death.

Normal USMC doctrine for patrols like this was to spread out the Marines on line so a single RPG or grenade couldn't take out the entire squad.

Since we were invading Z territory, though, and they hadn't shown inclinations of using firearms ("Yet," Sanchez had muttered ominously), Gunny modified our spread a bit.

On point walked Dominguez, our silent kill expert. The kid was proving to be an excellent Marine, his eyes sharp and alert, his posture relaxed, not jumpy. He was comfortable with the authority his role gave him, which was when he held up his fist, we all stopped.

We stopped a lot.

The rest of us walked in a loose group behind him, with Sanchez watching the rear. We scanned every car as we walked, careful not to disturb anything that might give us away. If something triggered the Zs, and they started flooding this way, we were going to be in the worst place possible.

Of course, halfway over this third-of-a-mile-long hunk of concrete, is when the horrible thought occurred to me: zombies didn't need a reason from us to flood over this bridge. They could just *do* it, and if they did, we were screwed.

I dropped back toward Gunny Hudson and shared the thought. His mouth set in a grim line.

"We're in it now, Sergeant. Let's just make the best of it."

"It's my fault," I muttered. "I should have thought of it

first."

Gunny grunted. "Really? Should have thought of it? And how were you going to magic us across the river without using one of these bridges?"

He scanned a nearby bus as we walked by. "Don't second-guess yourself, Slaughter. We're all here together, walking the same line, and if someone had thought it a danger, they would have called you out on it. That's the beauty of having a Corps of Marines."

"Whew," came the sound from our right. We both looked over to see TSgt Russell walking along, his head rocked back slightly. "The Corps sounds nice."

He grinned suddenly. "Oh, wait, that's right. I'm Air Force. My life is *so* much better."

I couldn't help it. The controller's humor got a smile out of me. "Whatever, man."

"Hey, you jarheads got friendship and stuff, but my chow hall's got a cheesecake line and my issued moisturizer smells like rainforest dew."

"Dude. I hate you."

"Aw."

****

As darkness draped over the cityscape, we stumbled off the bridge without incident, thank God.

"Moonbeams, Marines. Red lens only; Zulu's vision might be bad, but I'm pretty sure he can see bright lights in the dark," Gunny said, and Alpha circled up, digging in their packs.

'Moonbeam' is the Corps way of saying 'flashlights'. In a tactical environment where we didn't want to be seen, we'd screw red lens filters over the moonbeam light. It's harder to see red light from a distance as opposed to a bright white light.

"Kinda weird," Sanchez said, adjusting her aching shoulders as she clipped her moonbeam to her strap. "Wouldn't you think Zulu would be all over the place, especially in D.C.? I thought we said there was gonna be a couple million of them here; that's why we're being so quiet."

"If a tree falls in the forest and no one's around..." Dominguez said.

"What the freak does that mean?" Sanchez fired back.

"No, he's right," Gunny said. "Just because there should be a few million Zs around doesn't mean they're evenly distributed through the city. We might be making some noise, but if the horde is somewhere else, we're gonna be okay."

He looked at each of us. "These are trigger-based animals that move in swarms. They hear sound, they follow it like a school of fish. I think it's more likely that when we see our first Z, we're also going to see a million others."

"Cool," Ferreira said. Our other SAW gunner rubbed at his deltoid, and I didn't blame him. He and Sanchez had been carrying squad assault weapons this whole time, and that took a toll on your back. "Can you tell us why we took the long way now?"

"Don't need to," Hudson said, looking up. "We're there."

The Marines craned their necks back to see what he was looking at, and as the dim red beams played across the statue, I realized where we were.

The iconic image of Marines ramming a flag into the ground soared above us, set on a platform of black granite standing ten feet tall. The bronze statue itself was around thirty feet tall, not counting the flagpole.

"The Iwo Jima Memorial," I said quietly.

The Marines went quiet as we looked at this piece of our history. The flag still drooped from the end of the flagpole, swaying in the weak wind. Somehow, amid all the devastation we had already seen, this seemed untouched.

"On February 19, 1945," Gunny said, "the 4th and 5th Marine Divisions assaulted the black beaches of Iwo Jima. The imperial Japanese tore into them with focused machine gun fire and artillery. Casualties were astronomical, but the Marines didn't stop. The Japanese refused to retreat or surrender; *bushido* drove them to fight to the last man, which meant our brothers fought through a storm of lead, fire and blades. They started with twenty-one thousand imperial defenders on that island, Marines, and only two hundred sixteen of them survived the battle. *That's* what the fighting was like."

He paced in front of the memorial. "The island was a strategic necessity; it would give America somewhere to land B-29s for bombings, resupply and aid missions all over the Pacific, not to mention denying the imperials a vital airstrip to launch attacks on our Navy. Defeat was not an option."

"After four days of the worst fighting of the war," Hudson went on, "Marines from Easy Company, 2nd Battalion, fought their way to the top of Mount Suribachi and raised the flag. The cheer from the troops below, Marines and Navy, was so loud that the Japanese thought they had lost. Horns blew and Marines roared at the sight of our flag flying in victory over the bloodiest battlefield in our recent memory."

He patted a hand on the stone of the memorial. "But this isn't that moment."

Ferreira, entranced by the story, blinked. "What? Whatchu mean, it's not?"

Hudson grinned at him. "Flag wasn't big enough to be seen from the rest of the island. The CO ordered a larger flag raised in its place later that day, which got photographed and sent all over the world. That second raising is the scene we see here now."

He tapped the plaque on the dais. "Read this. What's it say?"

"'Uncommon valor,'" Sanchez read, "was a common virtue.'"

Gunny Hudson looked at each of us in turn. I felt a thrill run through my body as his eyes met mine. "Tomorrow, we're going to raise a flag. We're going to send out a siren call to every Z in thirty miles to come get some, so that Americans trapped in their homes can evac to safety. This enemy does not know how to retreat or surrender. We can't inflict enough psychological damage on them to make them give up."

He clenched his fist. "Tomorrow, we're carrying on the legacy of Iwo Jima. But this time we're on our land, saving *our* people, against an enemy that refuses to run away."

Hudson looked up at the memorial, at the flag waving gently in the breeze. "Six Marines raised the flag on Iwo Jima."

He looked down at us and pointed. "Slaughter. Dominguez. Sanchez. Dakota. Ferreira. Hudson. Six Marines of us here, too."

Ferreira glanced over at Russell. "What about Air Force?"

The combat controller shrugged with an easy grin. "And one cameraman," he said, pointing at his chest. That drew a chuckle from Alpha.

"We're racking out here tonight," Gunny said. "Sleep in the shadow of our ancestors. Me and Sergeant got first firewatch. He'll hand out the rest of the watch assignments."

The Marines clambered up the big platform, Dom boosting each one up before getting a hand up himself. Each Marine chose a spot beneath the statue. "Big shadow," I heard Ferreira mutter, and Dom grunted in response.

Big shadow. No kidding.

Chapter 20 - PISS BREAK

Hours later, I woke up in the dark, gasping as a hand dug painfully into the meat of my shoulder. I grimaced as it ground into a pressure point and tried to sit up, but then I made out Dominguez's face, finger held to his lips. He met my eyes, then chucked his chin ever so slightly toward the bridge.

His fingers eased up, and as my eyes adjusted to the darkness, I saw what he saw.

Silhouettes. Hundreds of them with red eyes, shuffling through the gray of the coming dawn.

Slowly, carefully, I lifted my rifle from my chest, not letting the metal scrape on anything. Every Marine in the field sleeps with his weapon, anyways, but it would have been the height of stupidity not to remain armed in *this* environment.

Nearby, I could already see the other Marines of Alpha, kneeling silently, weapons trained on the horde. Each of us knelt on the raised dais on which the statue of Iwo Jima rested, which meant the flood of animate dead parted around us like a stream around a stone. The platform was huge, ten feet off the ground, so I wasn't worried about any danger to us.

Wait. My count was off by two.

Two Marines were missing.

I glanced over at Gunny, who met my fierce gaze with his own. I mouthed, *Sanchez and Dakota?*

He reached down, gripped his crotch and tugged up. *Pissing.*

You had to be kidding me. That was not good. As a female, Sanchez wouldn't piss around us. Dakota was probably with her as a battle buddy. That meant they were somewhere out there in the dark, pants down and afraid, when this massive herd wandered over.

The crowd grunted and muttered as it shambled along. If I made a sound to try to get a lock on their location, the horde would swarm the edge of the dais. Even if they couldn't reach us, they could still keep us from getting down and being sieged by zombies here wasn't my idea of a good time.

Gunny held his hand parallel to the deck, signaling for *calm*. Nearby, Ferreira swept the barrel of his 249 over the crowd, checking for any sign the Zs knew we were there.

The only thing saving us so far was the low light, but the sun was coming up and that was going to go away real quick.

My mind raced for a solution, but our SpecOps controller was way ahead of me.

Something clicked nearby, and I turned to see TSgt Russell aim something into the sky. An instant later, a streak of brilliant red shot into the darkness, making my eyes water with its radiance. The flare arced over the river, back toward the bridge, and as one, the crowd of Zs pivoted to see it. Some even started running, and that triggered the rest of them. With groans and snarls, the crowd stampeded toward the bridge, eager to find that light.

We heard the Howl start up in other places in the city.

Gunny clenched his hand into a fist, making the signal for *hold*. His eyes were locked onto something, but even with the flare burning in the sky, I couldn't make it out.

Fifteen seconds later, I saw them. Dakota and Sanchez staggered through the horde, dodging running zombies like wildebeests. The pair was literally groaning and grunting like Zs, swaying and staggering to blend in with the undead. But there were too many between them and the dais, and if they stopped their desperate act, they were gonna get noticed and torn apart.

His voice low, still under the noise floor of the Howl, Gunny said, "Not til I shoot."

He held out a hand to Dak and Sanchez, signaling for them not to shoot. The flare was burning out as it fell toward the river. Red light chased shadows back toward us as it dipped lower and lower.

We had probably fifty Zs around the dais still, with another two or three hundred out towards the bridge. I could see them a lot better now, because the sun was cresting over the horizon, just enough to make my eyes reset. That meant the Zs, unable to blink, were going to be useless for a while until their vision adjusted.

Which meant it was the perfect time to light these blind mother—

Hudson's M4 barked, and a Z toppled over, liquid spraying from its head. In less than a second, the gunny shot another, then another.

Blam blam blam.

Russell fired next, right after him. His accuracy was phenomenal as he dropped Z after Z with point-blank headshots, clearing everything in his immediate area in a pattern he'd clearly marked out already.

Like I had.

My rifle twitched between heads, laying down lead in a zig-zag pattern in my lane. Next to me, the Marines of Alpha opened up, the two SAWs chewing into the edges of the bridge mob.

For about three seconds, we had nearly stock-still targets as their decayed brains tried to figure out where the gunfire was coming from, and we maximized that advantage. All fifty zombies around the dais leaked the contents of their skulls onto the pavement now, dropped by precision accuracy.

But now they had our scent, and they were running at us.

"Keep it up, Marines!" I roared, and Alpha's weapons roared with me. The leaders in the horde slammed into the deck, twisting and falling as .556 ripped into them. Tracer rounds zipped through, tracking fiery lines across the approaching face of the mass. Zombies pitched over backwards as the storm of gunfire raked through them.

Twenty yards out. But Dak and Sanchez weren't moving with them, and the Zs were starting to notice the nonconformists.

"Dom!" I shouted. The Marine glanced over at me, his shoulders juddering as he took shot after shot. "You're with me in front!"

More shots, then, "Oorah, Sergeant!"

Ten yards out. Too many Zs were getting too close to my Marines.

"Gunny!" I yelled. "Keep them off us!"

I didn't hear him respond. Once the zombies hit five yards out, I jumped off the dais.

****

One of my favorite scenes from *The Two Towers* movie was when the hero and dwarf jumped onto the bridge in front of the gate that the Uruk-hai were knocking down. They slammed into the monsters and knocked them off, giving the king and his men enough time to shore up the gate and save everyone inside.

Theirs looked really cool, since every time they swung their sword or axe, something fell off the bridge.

Mine was different.

As soon as my boots kissed ground, my elbow descended, smashed into a zombie's rotten teeth and piledrived the corpse into the ground. I extended my rifle horizontally and shoved with all of my weight snapping forward, and three or four more Zs flew backward, tangling up their buddies' legs as they fell.

I was wearing my cammies field-style, which meant I hadn't rolled my sleeves. No bare skin. I was putting a lot of faith in fabric right now as I lunged forward, gripped a Z just under its snapping jaw, and threw the thing as hard as I could crosswise into the mass.

For about a second, three yards of rushing Zs were stymied. In that second, a SAW can do a lot of damage. A line of fire stitched across the chests of the Zulus in front of me.

A zombie ran up on me, howling for my blood, and I planted the heel of my combat boot in its gut. The body had been dead and decomposing two days; it didn't handle a Spartan kick from a corn-fed Texas boy too well. Something foul exploded out of its pants, then a bullet took it in the face.

I caught sight of Dom, running interdiction with me. His grandpa's Ka-Bar drooled black blood as he rammed a knee into a zombie, stabbed its spine and twisted it away into another three of them.

This worked for about four seconds, then the weight of the horde told. I got hit by two of them at once, then eight more slammed into their backs. I kept my forearms up, trying to keep their snarling maws away from my neck as I backed up. It was hard to keep my footing, with all the bodies around, and I knew that if I went off my feet, I was joining the crowd in seconds. Weapons cracked off above me, and zombies hit the deck.

"We got 'em!" Gunny roared. "Slaughter, Dominguez, we got 'em! Get back!"

Thank God. Sanchez and Dakota had made it. I surged forward, slamming an elbow into a Z's jawline and sloughing off the two trying to eat me. I threw myself backward, and my heel hit the concrete of the dais.

"Jump, Sergeant!" someone shouted, and I extended both arms straight up and jumped as high as I could. Hands gripped my arms and hauled me up even as dead hands tried to grab my boots. I fell backward to roll to my stomach on the platform.

"Dom!" I shouted, my eyes scanning the horde.

There.

The kid fought like a banshee, but they'd cut him off. Ferreira had his SAW ripping away at the Zs behind him, and Dom kept backing up into that void. I didn't know how Furry was doing it, but not a single 5.56 hit his Marine Corps brother. The man was an artist with a machine gun.

Russell snapped his rifle over and added his fire to Ferreira's. A Zulu trying to chomp at Dom's neck screeched as blood exploded from its spine. Dom staggered backward, almost to the dais, and then his heel caught a Z's outstretched arm.

With a flail of his arms, Dom went down as the horde surged forward.

I didn't even think twice. I took one step and launched myself toward him. Two hundred sixty pounds of warfighter smashed into the Zulu tribe, tearing them off of my fallen Marine. I hit the deck and rolled, my hands lashing out in backhanded swipes to clear as much space as possible.

On the ground, Dom twisted up, gripped one of his attackers around the waist with his legs and threw the zombie from his feet. The Marine followed his own momentum, rolled to his feet, snapped a Z's knee backwards with a mule kick, took two steps and threw himself toward the dais. Russell and Dakota pulled him up.

Good. He was clear.

I jabbed the first Z in front of me, punching its nose into its face. Another grabbed my arm and sank its teeth into my extended arm. I roared, jerked my arm out of its mouth and shattered its jaw with probably the strongest roundhouse I've ever thrown. Gunfire slashed in front of me, and I threw myself backward as Ferreira and Sanchez dumped their box mags point-blank into the horde.

And then, just like that, it ended.

Dakota's rifle cracked once or twice more, dropping stragglers. I barely noticed. All I could hear was the blood pounding in my ears as I pulled at the sleeve of my bitten arm.

My fingers fumbled at the button and my vision blurred. *No, no, no.*

Then Gunny Hudson was there, M9 in his left hand. With one deft move, he undid the button on my sleeve with his free right hand, while simultaneously forcing the barrel of that pistol into my mouth.

"Don't move, Sergeant," he ordered, his tone grim as Death.

I relaxed and put my hands behind my back slowly. In fact, I adjusted the angle of my head to fit the angle of the gun barrel better. If this was it, I wanted to be gone immediately.

With a tug, Hudson jerked the sleeve up off my forearm. I didn't look; I just closed my eyes.

After a second, the barrel of the gun eased out of my mouth. "You're clean, Sergeant," Hudson said, letting out a huge breath. "Skin's not broken. Cammies saved you."

I felt weak, and reached out for the dais. "Zulu needs to take better care of his teeth," I said, and Hudson grinned. The relief between us was *thick*.

"Appreciate the save, Gunny," I said quietly. "And the check-up."

Hudson shrugged as he holstered his sidearm. "Not the first time we've tasted gun in the wee hours of the morning."

I chuckled at the dark humor. "Do this a few more times, won't be the last, either. That reminds me. Dom!"

"Yeah, Sergeant?"

"You good?"

Russell was checking him, and the controller gave me a thumbs up. The lance corporal groaned and cracked his neck. "Yeah, Sergeant. But I got questions about my leadership's decision-making matrix."

I chuckled. "Save it for the monthly mental assessment, devil."

"Which are anonymous, yet somehow required," Ferreira said.

"'Anonymous,'" Dakota said, fingers in air quotes.

"Sanchez," I said. "You good? You get your piss?"

Sanchez rolled her eyes and flopped to the side. "Nah, Sergeant. I think I've decided to hold it."

Chapter 21 - POURING ONE OUT

We ate a solid breakfast of MRE on the move, half of us sporking cold vegetable lasagna from the packet while the others kept their eyes up. We hiked parallel to the 110 South, which took us through Arlington National Cemetery. The Iwo Jima Memorial, also called the United States Marine Corps War Memorial, rested at the extreme north of the graveyard, and our destination lay on the other side.

The grass was green and lush beneath our feet, remnants of dew still clinging to the verdant blades. As far as the eye could see, green fields with white gravestones stretched out.

Dakota sniffled, and I glanced over at him. "What's up, devil?"

He gestured out at the fields. "I mean, look at this, Sergeant. This is the history of American warfare. United States heroes are buried out here. Every one of these guys out there fought for freedom, to make our country what it is."

His eyes fell. "I feel like they're watching me, Sergeant. Guys who jumped on grenades for their squad or out of a boat on D-Day are looking down on me, and man, I feel like I'm going to let them down."

I chuckled. "Well, you're *not* with these guys, cuz you aren't dead yet, but I think you need to look at it from their point of view."

"Yeah?" Ferreira put in. "How's that?"

I glanced back at him, and I saw the concern hiding behind the bravado and swagger. The same look, in one form or another, hidden different ways on Sanchez and Dom. I knew that feeling. Every Marine does. Every Marine has the terror lurking inside, the panic waiting to bust out because *I'm going to fail my brothers.*

Every Marine is trained to think of the Marines who went on before. Our ancestors, not through genetics but blood, who fought the battles of their times and emerged victorious.

"You think they're better than you?" I asked.

All four of them, Sanchez, Dominguez, Ferreira and Dakota, nodded in unison. "Yeah," Sanchez said. "These guys were heroes."

"Hm," I said. "Better question. Do you think *they think* they're better than you?"

That brought them up short. Our boots pounded the grass in silence for a minute until I spoke again.

"D-Day," I said. "That was big. Rushing a shore bristling with German guns. Or Gettysburg, marching up a hill with cannons and rifles cracking down at you. Iwo Jima. Inchon. Hue City."

I stabbed a finger down as we walked. "You think Washington D.C. is going to be smaller than that?"

"What?" Dakota said, blinking.

Gunny laughed at his reaction. "You killers really have no idea of the crazy plan you came up with. Once Dakota turns on that signal, every hostile in a hundred miles is coming right for us. That numbers in the millions, maybe even tens of millions."

"By comparison," I said, "D-Day had maybe a million and a half combatants. The Spartans at Thermopylae had a few hundred against hundreds of thousands."

I circled my hand above my head. "And we're seven, taunting ten million flesh-eating monsters after us so the Navy can conduct an evacuation that makes Dunkirk look like a warm-up."

Gunny clapped Dakota on the back. "Don't sweat what they think of you, devil. When Zulu finally takes us down, the American heroes here will be lining up to shake your hand."

****

A few minutes later, I snagged Dakota and drew him to the side.

"Inspirational manure aside," I said, "Does the Navy know

they're about to get a crap ton of civilians running towards them once the Zs start heading towards us?"

Dakota scratched at his neck. His stubble was probably getting itchy by now. "So, Cavanaugh says there's Navy guys in the FEMA tent. Whitney has been having conferences with our Colonel Santiago, Colonel Bauer from that deploying Marine battalion, and Admiral Jenkins commanding local Naval forces. Apparently, Whitney's trying to assert his authority over them and they are reluctant to accede to it until it's confirmed that the political chain of command has been annihilated."

"So...?" I asked.

Dakota sighed. "Cavanaugh says he's talked to sailors who came with the admiral. Right now, the ships are still around Kent Island and Colonel Bauer's Marines are still holding those bridges, so they're technically ready to receive civilians, even if they don't know that they're coming yet. Cavanaugh says they're not moving yet because the admiral and Bauer are real pissed off with Whitney."

I shook my head as Gunny came up next to me. "This whole thing is off," I said. "Whitney's throwing a lot of weight around, but he's not actually doing his job."

I glanced at Dakota. "Can I talk to Cavanaugh?"

The Marine checked his watch. "Sure thing. Next comm window is coming up now."

"'Comm window'? What's that mean?" Gunny asked.

Dakota pulled out his radio and started fiddling with it as I signaled for a halt. "Cavanaugh's taking smoke breaks. Apparently, Whitney hates the smell, so he never goes near the smoke pit."

I rolled my eyes. "Yeah, that tracks."

Dakota handed me the headset. "Here you go, Sergeant. Don't worry about protocol; we haven't been using it between us."

I put the set on. "We good?"

Dakota gave me a thumbs up. At the same time, I heard,

"You're good, Sergeant."

"This Lance Corporal Cavanaugh?"

"Oorah, Sergeant. Dylan says you got some questions for me?"

I wracked my brain before remembering Dakota's first name was Dylan. "Yeah, couple of things. How many people actually know what we're trying to do out here?"

"I hear you on that. So far, I've spread the word among all the lower enlisted guys I've run into, other than the suck-ups who would tell on us, and we're all in agreement. We're keeping things low-key for now until there's no way anyone can cancel the op."

I pressed my lips together. "You sure that's the way to go? It's our butts on the line out here."

"With respect, Sergeant, you haven't been hearing the arguments I have. Whitney is screaming at our command, saying they are legally obligated to swear their loyalty to him like he's some kind of dictator. They're saying that they're here to save as many civilians as possible, not serve as Whitney's private army. You do not yet want to be a part of this argument."

I glanced at Gunny, who nodded. "Aight, I'm trusting you on that. We're about an hour out from the broadcast point. Dakota, how long to set up your squirrel stuff to get the signal ready to go?"

Dakota chewed on his lip. "Maybe two hours, factoring in Murphy's Law?"

"You hear that, Lance Corporal?" I said into the mic. "You're looking at three hours to get that signal ready to go. Every phone, every tablet, drawing every Z away from suburban areas and channeling them toward us."

"Kill, Sergeant," came the response. *"Program is already coded and ready to run, and civilians have already had prep messages sent to their phones. Once I hit Send, every smart device with power in east D.C. is going to activate and send out the emergency signal at max volume. The sound itself is a*

high-pitched squeal, beyond our hearing range. I stashed one on a supply chopper as a test, and it drove Zs beneath the chopper nuts. You should have seen them running after it like it was a gut truck.

"Me and a couple other guys that flunked out of college math also already factored in zombie run times, based on footage of them moving at hunting speed. Once the average zombie is calculated to hit the phone, the next one will activate, stringing them along through the city til they hit the airport you're set up at. Volume on the squeal will fade on phones nearest the horde, while the furthest one will be max volume."

I chuckled. "Marine, if this works and we're somehow still alive, I'm putting you in for a NAM."

"Ooo, a whole Navy Achievement Medal, just for me? Not likely. For all this Pied Piper crap, I want my own parade."

"I'll see what I can do. Get back to work before I write you up for malingering."

"Errah, Sergeant. Have fun."

"Heard. Out."

I took off the headset and handed it back to Dakota. "Okay, I'm satisfied. We have a high probability of civilians having someplace to go, a medium likelihood of getting some air support, and a basically-zero chance of living through the rest of today."

"Cool," Ferreira said. "Drinks are on me afterwards, then."

"Nice," Sanchez said, socking him in the shoulder. "Now I'm going to make sure you live."

****

The last thing we saw before hitting the airport probably sobered us the most.

"Hey, crayon-eaters," Russell said.

We glanced at him, and he pointed. "Check it out."

We looked where he was pointing, and Ferreira let slip an

F-bomb before glancing at Gunny sheepishly. "Sorry, Gunny."

"Keep control of yourself," Hudson said sternly, but even he looked rocked by the sight before us.

The Pentagon, the once grand temple of the American military machine, now crumbled in ruins, its walls blackened and charred as smoke rose in grey pillars from its corpse. The windows were shattered, the metal doors twisted and mangled. Cars lay in the parking lot like bodies, uniformly gray and black. Grey hung over the desolate scene, casting hazy shadow over the desolation.

The air tasted thick and stale, with a sickly aroma of decay mixed with the acrid smell of chemicals. Ash and death filled the air, carried on a poisoned wind and leaving a bitter aftertaste on our tongues.

We could see lurching figures even in the smoke, stumbling around the flame-ravaged rubble of the Pentagon. The eerie silence was broken only by the creaking and groaning of the weakened structure, with occasional crashing sounds from within as some floor gave way and the Howl of the dead surged once again.

I blew my breath out slowly. Three days ago, it had been the fortress of American power, the altar of our arrogance. We had been untouchable, powerful and divine.

Now it stood only as a husk of its glory, a haunting reminder of the world we had lost, infested with the moaning parasites who had torn it down.

"Keep moving," Gunny said, and we hiked up our packs onto our shoulders, somber at the sight.

"Man," Ferreira said. "I didn't think about this before, but... you think we're still getting paid?

Sanchez hit him again. "Shut up, man."

Chapter 22 – THE FIRST GENERAL ORDER

"So that's it, huh?"

An hour later, the seven of us were looking at the Ronald Reagan National Airport. Describing it from east to west, the runways were backed by the Potomac River, running in parallel with the terminals that fell in a straight line away from us. Railroad tracks curved down a few hundred yards beyond that, and just on the other side of those was US-1, also known as Jefferson Davis Highway or Richmond Highway, depending on where you were from. Buttressing the highway were various office buildings, restaurants and parking garages.

The airport itself wasn't that big. The surprising thing was that the air traffic control tower rose from the roof of the terminal itself, not set back on the runways. It gave a commanding view of the parking lot, runways and all government property in view.

Beside me, Russell muttered, "I like this."

I glanced at him as he gestured toward the airport. "I set up in the tower with my designator, and I get all this open ground to target airstrikes and naval bombardment. This is a serious kill zone here."

He slapped me on the shoulder. "Nice pick, jarhead."

I grinned at him. "Want a lawn chair while you're up there?"

He raised an eyebrow at me. "Got one available?"

I moved over to Dakota. "What's your plan?"

He rubbed the scratch on his chin. "Look, this place is a nightmare. Check this out."

He pointed. "The airport is a rectangle, right? And the long end faces the city. The entire back end of the airport facing the river is glass. There are multiple terminals, which means multiple entry points on this long end."

I nodded. "Yeah, it's a defensive nightmare. Probably couldn't hold this place with a hundred Marines, much less six and a hobbyist."

"I heard that," Russell growled.

With a slight smile, I chucked my chin at Dakota. "So, what's the solution?"

He ticked a finger toward the tower.

"I think I should go with Air Force. Tower's got height, should have the connections I need and the antenna, not to mention a controlled entry point. Only way in is at the bottom."

"I only got one chair, kid...."

Gunny moved closer. "I still want to use the airport as a firebreak," he said thoughtfully. "Zs can get stuck inside, we tear 'em up. We can hold out longer."

I clapped Dakota on the back. "Good thinking, devil. Let's go get you set up."

"Sanchez, Dominguez, Ferreira," Gunny said. "Head inside and clear out any Zs wandering around, quietly if you can. We don't want any party guests showing up before the music starts. Lance Corporal Dominguez, you're in charge. And make sure you close and lock as many doors as possible. I want this place as sealed as we can get it in two hours."

Dom nodded. "Oorah, Gunny."

The three of them broke off and jogged toward the terminal.

"Sergeant, you accompany Dakota on his squirrel mission. Get those emitters placed and his hub operational. Two hours, Marines."

I nodded and checked my rifle. "You got it, Gunny. What about you?"

He indicated Russell. "I'm going with Air Force here and getting him set up. Tech Sergeant Russell is our biggest chance to walk out today, so I'm going to make sure he's super comfy and secure."

Russell grinned and tipped his boonie cover. "Comfiness *is* a major operational concern. Appreciate it, Gunny."

****

The tower had a… unique look to it.

"Looks like a bunch of paper cups stacked on top of each other," Dakota muttered, and I had to agree. It was a white column with almost a corrugated aesthetic, soaring into the sky above the weirdly curved roof. The style of the roof itself was a bunch of gentle curves like the waves of the ocean.

It was a five-minute jog to the tower. We arrowed straight for the main terminal, leaving any potential building clear to Dom's fireteam. The entrance would probably be just inside the terminal itself, with some locks between us and the tower control.

Before going inside, Dominguez and his team came to a halt and we pulled alongside them. Dom threw some hand commands, smartly avoiding unnecessary sound, and Sanchez and Ferreira split off to take up positions on the entrance while Dom dropped his pack, slung his rifle around his back and drew his Ka-Bar.

That kid had really grown a lot over the past few days. I watched him roll his shoulders once, then vanish into the dimness of the terminal. There was a confidence to him that hadn't been there before, and I couldn't help but feel some pride.

All Marines have swagger. We get it the instant we graduate boot camp and pin that eagle, globe and anchor on our collars. But there's still that hesitation, that anxiety that once combat hits, you're not going to be enough.

Dom had lost that. He disappeared into that possibly infested terminal without hesitation, without even a backward look or a fist bump with his Marines. He was all business, looking for Zulus to drop so his Marines would be safe.

"Kill, Marine," I whispered.

"Give him a minute," I said to Dak. "We'll go in once he's cleared the entranceway."

"Oorah, Sergeant. Better him than me," Dakota answered.

Something choked inside, trying to gasp out the Howl through its now-ruined throat. "Well, he's better *at it* than you," I said, and Sanchez and Ferreira chuckled.

****

I gave Dom ten minutes to do his thing without distraction. Last thing I wanted to do was bust in too early and screw up one of his takedowns.

I led the way into the airport terminal, rifle raised and finger on the trigger. As I slid through the doors, heel-toeing to reduce sound, I kept my eye glued to my RCO. It took a second for my eyes to adjust to the difference in lighting, and on the floor, I saw several Zs crumpled on the ground.

"Jeez, what was this dude's grandpa, a Shinobi?" Dakota muttered.

I tapped him on the shoulder to shut him up, and he nodded.

We sidestepped over a couple bodies and came up to a sealed door.

"Yep," Dakota said quietly, examining a keypad next to the door. "Coded entry."

I grunted bitterly. *Had to be something.*

"Can you get in?"

Dak pulled out his radio. "Not yet. I bet somebody can, though."

He clicked the mic twice.

About thirty seconds later, I heard Cavanaugh's voice. *"Operator."*

Dakota held the radio close to his mouth and said, "You were right. Tower door's key carded. Did you find that emergency unlock code yet?"

"Does the pope poop in the woods?"

Dakota grinned and responded, "I guess we're about to find out."

Ten seconds later, he tapped in a sequence on the pad and

something in the heavy door clicked. He hauled the door open and gestured. "After you, mon sergeant."

I sighed and moved past him.

Lances.

****

The interior of the tower was a bank of consoles, screens and headsets. Along one side rested a table with a coffeemaker on it, along with some phone chargers plugged into a power strip. A couple of the cords were pink.

I squinted at that. "You'd think they couldn't have phones in here."

"Oh, yeah, Sergeant," Dak said, already crouching down to check some connections. "Nobody in comms ever breaks the no-phone reg."

"Lance Corporal, get to work before you admit to a felony I'll have to report you for."

He was wriggling under the console when he answered, "Aye, Sergeant."

To this day, I have no idea what that kid did. It took him an hour of muttering and swearing as he made connections, remade them, spliced wires, tapped at keyboards and called Cavanaugh for advice.

Apparently, the entire S6 was in on our scheme, because I kept hearing different voices coming through the radio, offering varying shades of advice and arguing with each other.

Whatever. The S6 was basically the Mafia, and they don't rat on nobody. Besides, everything was about to go down anyways.

I've learned since then that Dakota's 'creative repurposing' of the control tower's broadcast capability was nothing short of Einstein-level brilliance, and top government experts still have no idea just how he did what he did.

It did not seem brilliant at the time as I watched him chew on a boot band and hammer his palm against the side of a monitor while loudly theorizing on its maker's mother's probable promiscuity.

Finally, he leaned back in his chair, took his abused boot band out of his mouth and announced, "Sergeant, we have ignition."

I blew out the breath I'd been holding and radioed Gunny. "Gunny, Pied Piper is a go."

"*Roger that,*" came the response. "*Air Force heading your way for the height. We're making ready to receive down here.*"

I clicked the mic. "What, he didn't like his chair?"

Russell's voice came over the net. "*I like yours better.*"

"Whatever. Ten four."

I clipped the handset back to my shoulder strap and sighed. "Aight. I'm heading downstairs to help them set up and repel. You need anything from me?"

"No, Sergeant," he said. "As long as you guys are ready for wave one, we're good."

My brain stopped at that. "Hold up, what now? What's wave one?"

After two minutes of his explanation, I radioed Hudson. "Gunny, we're about to have a problem."

****

"He said what?" Sanchez hissed. The five of us gathered in the terminal in front of the stairwell door that led into the tower. Dom had finished his sweep a bit before, and had already cleaned and sheathed his blade.

I heaved a deep breath. "The system functions like a siren call. The tower's going to broadcast at the same time as the phones in a massive radius, so that Zs running our way get caught in its net. Dak says it's the best way to make sure they stay locked onto us and not civilians trying to evac."

Gunny rubbed the bridge of his nose. "But that also means every Zulu already in its radius will head here first."

I nodded. "Exactly. Wave one."

"But we're getting air strikes, right?" Ferreira asked. "Like, we can still bomb the crap out of them still, right?"

"Theoretically," I said. "Tech Sergeant's up there now, coordinating with his people at Langley Air Force Base. He seems to think everything's in order."

"Question," Dominguez said, raising his hand.

"What are you, in fourth grade?" Ferreira asked. "Put your hand down."

"Yo, shut up," Dom retorted, and turned back to me. "Why can't we just turn the signal on and leave? The Zs come here either way. Just lock the door to the tower and leave, right?"

I shook my head. "Dak says the system's finicky. He has to monitor it to keep the signal from glitching out. If that broadcast cuts when civilians are in the open running for Kent Island, it's going to be bad news."

Dom nodded and leaned back.

"So what I'm hearing," Ferreira said, "is lock Dakota up there and we can all leave."

Sanchez smacked him in the back of the head. "No Marine left behind, *cabron*. Do you even Marine, bro?"

"Don't even give me that. You'd leave me behind in a Mexican minute."

"A Mexican minute? That different from white minutes somehow?"

"I dunno, my burrito's always cold, so *something's* wrong...."

"If you Marines are finished," Gunny said with a look that meant they *were* finished, "take a knee and let's run over the plan for wave one."

As Marines lowered themselves to one knee, Gunny said, "Now Lance Corporal Dakota thinks his beacon will reach up to a mile away. That means that every Zulu within a mile radius of this place is going to start sprinting its way here."

Sanchez blew out her breath. "How many *is* that?"

Gunny chuckled once and waved a hand. "It's so many, it's not even worth thinking about. Now Tech Sergeant Russell has dedicated air support with squadrons from Langley Air Force Base. They held their runways and have been flying sorties to support troops on the ground, so maybe we'll get some love from there. We have assurances from Lance Corporal Cavanaugh that the Navy is prepared to receive the civilians coming in. Once we turn this signal on, the cat's out of the bag and hopefully we'll get some support from Navy and Marine units, as well."

He looked each of us in the eye. "Do not misunderstand me, Marines. As great as it sounds to have all this support, it's us frontlining it. There are six Marines and one Air Force combat controller to defend a multi-acre facility that is essentially a single giant entrance. Do not get stupid. Our bombs'll kill you just as easy as it kills Zulu. We are here to pick off stragglers that manage to live through the hell the Air Force is about to drop on them, not solo all of undead D.C., am I understood?"

"Aye, Gunny," they said.

Hudson cocked his head at me. "Sergeant Slaughter. I didn't hear you."

I blinked, a little surprised at being singled out. "Aye, Gunny."

He pointed at me. "You're the one who keeps throwing himself into crowds of cannibals, Sergeant. You're the one I'm worried about. Set the example."

I clenched my jaw, but I knew he was right. "Understood, Gunnery Sergeant."

"Yeah, Sergeant," said Ferreira. "Don't you know Marine Corps leaders should get eaten last?"

I thumped him on the Kevlar.

Gunny pointed at the runways behind the airport. "That's the Potomac. I'm reasonably certain Zulus still can't swim, so we have a single one eighty degree arc from which the horde will come. This facility is not a fortress; it's designed to be entered by large numbers of people, so don't be surprised when that happens. If you have to fall back, do it by bounds and toward the center of the terminal. Then we'll fall back as a group toward the river, got it?"

"Oorah, Gunny," we chorused.

"Watch your ammo consumption. Let the Air Force's bombs do the work. There will be no paperwork if you wind up bringing rounds back to base."

They chuckled at that.

"This enemy," Gunny said with the glint of steel in his eye, "has never been fought to a standstill, not in its numbers. The Army fell back. The Navy fell back. The rest of the Corps fell back. The Z has always won when in numbers, and we have always run. Not today. We're drawing the line here."

He let out a deep growling breath, and his hands gripped that Benelli M1014 shotgun. "And we're going to kill so many of them, college kids in history classes will never believe there were only seven of us."

Chapter 23 - COMBAT CONTROL FREAK

The wind blew through the parking lot outside, taking leaves, wrappers and some plastic bags with it. The manicured trees swayed in that breeze. I could smell the salt of the ocean, hear the flow of the river behind us.

I checked my Marines one last time, jogging down the terminal. Sanchez anchored the south end with her SAW, supported by Dom. Gunny and I would hold the center and Ferreira would hold the north. Dakota and Russell would be in the tower.

The ammo situation was not great for the SAWs. Ferreira and Sanchez had been through several heavy engagements already without resupply. They'd managed to snag some ammo from an overrun guard post at the Capitol, but not much.

And when the SAWs went dry, we were going to be up Zulu Creek without a paddle.

I didn't say any of this out loud. The strength of the Corps's lance corporals is that they think they can do anything. We have a belief in our invincibility at that level of experience. It makes the E-3 corps absolutely savage fighters, and I wasn't going to take that from them.

Not in their final moments.

I knew it. And I saw it in Gunny's eyes, too.

We were going to die here, lost in a tide of undead flesh, giving our lives so Americans could make it to safety.

One thing left to do.

I hit my radio. "Dak."

The response came back. "*Sergeant*?"

"Hit it."

****

I didn't hear a thing. I thought I would. I figured there would be some kind of high-pitched keening, something to make me grit my teeth or get a headache.

I clicked my mic. "Uh… did you hit it?"

"Yeah, it's going, and Cav's got his running, too," came the irritated response. *"Why?"*

I shrugged, sweating in my cammies. "No reason. I just thought—"

Then I heard the response, and the sound clamped my lips shut.

It rose from the city in front of us. It came from across the river behind us. It was the Howl, but amplified like I'd never heard it before. It rose like a roar all around us, unceasing and overwhelming. Birds launched into the sky, even the carrion feeders desperate to flee what was coming for us, as the first silhouettes appeared, sprinting right for us.

I let out a breath. "And here… we… go."

They burst from the city, the undead that still lurked in Arlington. The door of a Subway exploded into shards of glass as zombies lurched out of it. More glass shattered as corpses spilled out of buildings, their eyes and mouths wide. Even from this distance, I could see the red gazes, staring and frenzied.

Dakota's signal had kicked the roach nest, and the insects were swarming towards us.

I hit my radio. "Heads up. First customers incoming."

Next to me, Gunny clicked onto the net. "Remember, Marines. They're gonna trickle at first as the closest ones come for us, then they'll get more dense as the streets funnel them in. Conserve your ammo."

Furry's voice came over. *"Hey, Sanchez, you qualify expert?"*

"You asking cuz I'm a girl?"

"Sorta."

"Yeah, I did. Did you?"

"I'm not a girl, so obviously."

"No one thinks that's obvious, Furry."

We let them talk. Russell was on a different frequency, and

it would keep these kids frosty for what was coming.

"Boss?"

That was Dom. "Yeah, go ahead," I said.

"I don't hear jets."

I glanced outside. We still had a few hundred yards, so about two minutes before contact.

"I'll check."

I raised Dakota. "Ask Air Force when's support showing up, please."

"Uh...."

I raised an eyebrow. I didn't like the sound of that. Gunny shifted next to me, a frown on his face. "What's 'uh' mean, Lance Corporal?"

A second of nothing, then, *"Switch to command net, please."*

Outside, Zs bounded for us in long, loping strides. I switched to the preset for the link to Command, a pit forming in my stomach.

"—ck do you mean, strike authorities have been revoked? Who authorized that? Do you have any idea what's inbound to my position right now?"

Oh, man. Russell sounded *pissed.*

"Tech Sergeant, as previously stated, all strikes have been diverted away from your position and squadrons grounded. This has been confirmed on direct order from the highest authority."

I jammed my thumb on the transmit button so hard, I think I almost broke it. "This is Sergeant Slaughter, 2nd Marine Division. We're about to be engaged by every active hostile in three cities. What's the malfunction?"

A moment, then a grim *"Stand by, Sergeant."*

Stand by? Stand by for w—?

"Sergeant Slaughter. You know, Dr. Morano said you'd still be alive."

My blood froze. "Whitney," I growled.

"That's Acting President Whitney to you, soldier. Did you

really think I wouldn't find out all the resources you're trying to take away from me? Did you think I wouldn't know?"

"I'm trying to save American civilians, you pathetic—"

He cut me off. *"I don't care what some high school dropout with a gun thinks. These planes, these ships, and every man and woman on them: they're all mine. I need a strong core to rebuild this country around, and I'm not spending any of it to help some traitor to my new nation."*

A shot rang out. A zombie hit the deck, tumbling as its brains leaked out of the new hole in its head. There were more behind it. A lot more.

"Is that understood?" His voice sounded a little more distant, and I knew he was addressing the bridge of whatever Naval vessel he was on. *"There will be no assets diverted to this little treasonous errand."*

"Marines," I yelled out. "No help coming! Move to engage! Keep them out of the tower!"

Roars of assent echoed through the airport and weapons cracked.

Gunny and I surged out of the terminal doors into the open where zombies, still in ones and twos, sprinted for us. Their mouths gaped and bloody drool spilled from their jaws as they lurched to intercept.

Gunny's shotgun barked and a Z flew backwards, its head and chest ravaged by buckshot. My M4 snapped off two shots, dropping another.

In my ear, Whitney had the mic on still. Idiot hadn't hit the off switch. I heard Colonel Santiago's voice, a lethal edge to it. *"I know I did not just hear that correctly. We're going to abandon Marines in combat?"*

"Is that a problem, soldier?" Whitney snapped. *"How about you follow orders and bark when I tell you to?"*

Rage pulsed through my veins, boiling my blood, and my vision reddened as I entered my kill state. Zs hit the deck as my weapon fired, each trigger pull a kill, but it wasn't enough for me. Shooting them wasn't enough.

My Marines were going to die because of some stuffed shirt's power play.

Gunny's shotgun roared non-stop, the semi-automatic weapon firing about once a second. That's how I knew how much time had passed, because his weapon ran dry the same time mine did. The difference was Gunny backed up to reload.

The second my trigger clicked empty, I rushed forward and slammed my rifle butt into the nearest zombie's face. It had been a female, small, lower muscle density than usual. I smashed it from its feet and kicked its skull in. I got a mag into my hand.

"Sir, with all due respect, we do not and will not abandon Marines—"

"Shut your mouth, colonel, or I'll have you removed from command. Captain, get this ship moving. Inform the admiral that I want this group in the ocean and moving north to establish a new base of operations."

Another voice, female. *"Sir, 3rd platoon is reporting civilian movement en masse toward the bridge to Kent Island. No hostiles in sight."*

A voice, deep and full of authority that I didn't recognize. *"Understood, lieutenant. Chief, make ready to receive survivors."*

Whitney again. *"Belay that order, captain, and get this naval group moving. We don't have food or time for passengers."*

"I beg your pardon, Whitney? I need you to repeat that, because it sounds like you just ordered us to abandon Americans who need our help."

Another female. *"Sir, Langley is requesting confirmation of the RTB order on their squadrons already in the air."*

"My title is Mr. President, you stupid prick! What is wrong with all of you?"

I heard Furry's SAW then, a long chatter of sustained rounds. I axed a Z in the head with the mag in my hand and twisted to see Ferreira raking his weapon across the face of the zombies rushing him. Zs twisted and fell all the way out to the highway, but more emerged from the city line, screaming without end.

On the south side, Dom and Sanchez were blasting Zulus away from their entrance point while above us all, Dakota sniped as best as he could from the control tower.

I wiped the mag off on my leg and rammed it into the mag well, reasonably sure there was no material on it that would make my weapon jam.

I had about twenty targets just in front me. I stepped forward, then an M9 barked behind me, unloading its magazine. Four Zs pitched backwards, sprays of blood jetting from their heads. As soon as Gunny's pistol ran dry, I crashed into the remainder and my mind vanished into the melee of combat.

Butt stroke, step back, double-tap skull, turn, barrel rake the hands off, shoot the knee, knee the skull, kick, double-tap, switch to his buddy, double-tap, step over crawler, turn and double-tap, turn and crotch-kick, jam barrel into head, double-tap, butt stroke, reverse butt stroke, duck Gunny's shotgun blast, sight in on one knee, double-tap, double—

In my ear, the war raged.

"—emergency powers grant me all authority here and I order you to withdraw, Captain!"

"Mr. President, I will not abandon American civilians when we can clearly offer aid, nor leave Marines engaged in combat when it is in my power to support! Your orders are unlawful and immoral, sir!"

"Mr. President, Langley wishes to speak with you directly."

"Enough! All of you, shut up! I am the President of these United States, so get this boat moving, or so help me God, I will have you all shot for treason and—"

A shot rang out.

It was enough to shock me out of my reverie, and I stumbled back, hand to ear, trying to make sense of it. That wasn't one of our weapons. It had come through the ear piece.

I reset, fired a couple more double-taps to clear space. "What was that?" Gunny yelled over at me.

Then a voice of malice and fury growled over the comm. *"Sergeant."*

I didn't recognize it for an instant, then a helpless grin broke over my face as it registered. I dumped four more shots out. "Sergeant Major, good to hear your voice."

"Acting President Whitney evidenced clear and unmistakable evidence of being infected by the biological contagion, and I have acted decisively to prevent spread to the ship. Lance Corporal Cavanaugh, check the body for bites, please."

A second passed. Gunny and I started backing up toward the airport.

"Uh, I don't see—"

"Lance Corporal. Right there on the ankle. Get closer."

"I still don't see— oh."

Then, very glumly, *"Aye, aye, Sergeant Major."*

"Captain, please take charge of this mission. Lance Corporal… go brush your teeth."

"Understood. Chief, inform the Navajo *to prepare to receive survivors; we're not moving until they are all on board. Marine elements will remain in place to escort civilians across the bridge. Inform* The Sullivans *and the* Arleigh-Burke *to prepare for shore bombardment. Lieutenant, inform* Langley *that the mission is back on."*

Then, *"Sergeant Slaughter, this is Captain Hayden."*

I pulled my mic. "Yes, Captain?"

"My apologies for the delay. Support is on the way."

Another voice broke over the net. Russell. *"Slaughter!"*

"Yeah?"

He was laughing.

"You're gonna wanna back up, man!"

****

"Marines!" I yelled into the net. "Disengage! Fall back to the terminal!"

Acknowledgements poured in as I turned and ran. "Moving!"

I'm up, they see me, I'm down.

Gunny's shotgun blasted twice in that time. I turned back and dropped to a knee. "Move!"

Gunny twisted and sprinted back toward me. I sighted in and dropped one, two more Zs. They were getting thicker now. The city streets had collected them and now they were pouring out in greater numbers toward us.

Then the thing I dreaded to hear. *"This is Furry. I'm out."*

"Drop the weapon and run!" I shouted. North side was vulnerable now. "Dom, get over to his position."

"Rah, Sergeant!"

Gunny and I bounded back to the terminal, dropping Zs every step of the way.

We backed inside, weapons barking non-stop. Zombies crashed to the deck, still howling, still clawing towards us.

"Russell!" I shouted. "We need those bombs!"

"For what yer about to receive," the controller answered, *"be sure and say thank you."*

Something roared overhead, and I saw the F-22 Raptor tilt and bank as it blasted past the airport.

And the first five-hundreds hit.

****

Six GBU-38 JDAMs hit the parking lot of the Reagan National Airport in a spread. I found out later those jets had just slowed down from the Mach 1.5 they used to reach us down to a reasonable bombing speed of six hundred MPH.

The five-hundred-pound bombs slammed into the concrete in a line parallel to the face of the terminal and detonated. Dirt and smoke geysered into the air as air blasted past me. At this distance, pressure waves weren't a concern, but my eardrums were. The Zs, on the other hand, blew apart within fifty yards of each bomb. Shards of concrete and body parts showered the parking lot around me.

"Marines," I shouted. "Inside, inside, inside!"

The next Raptor released its payload, and this time, they exploded mid-air, fifty feet above the hordes. Rains of shrapnel scythed through the Zs, dropping acres of the dead to the ground at once.

In the distance, buildings exploded as Naval 5-inch guns and Tomahawks slammed into their bases. Brick and glass blew out onto the street as they crumpled like they had been shot. The howl of Air Force fighter-bombers shrieking in drowned out the Howl of the Zulu tribe, blasting them back to their graves.

They told me later that the Air Force set the first JDAMs to hit the parking lot itself. They wanted to break up the concrete to slow the horde down. As a matter of fact, the Navy also fired their shore bombardment cannons at the streets for the same reason. I saw the satellite images later, and saw why.

D.C. was crawling like an anthill had been kicked. Whatever signal Dakota and Cavanaugh had cooked up had drawn millions of the dead to us. The Zulus flowed through the streets like a river of rotting flesh, drawn by Dakota's siren call directly to us.

I learned things about the US Air Force since that time.

Langley kept squadrons on emergency call at all times. When the apocalypse hit, those airmen moved to secure their runways and get their jets in the air. Since that time, they had repulsed constant attacks by the undead and kept their jets active. They had three squadrons of twenty F-22s each. Those F-22s could launch ten at a time every five minutes.

It took seven minutes to reach Reagan National Airport from Langley Air Force Base at a speed of Mach 1.5 to release their racks of bombs. Then a seven-minute flight back to Langley, boosting back to supersonic. It took Langley's ground crews half an hour to reload and refuel each jet.

Forty-five-minute turnaround on each aircraft. Just on the F-22s.

That didn't even include the random A-10s that kept showing up, or the Naval jet fighters, or the Naval guns themselves.

The United States military obliterated the half-mile just outside the airport for five hours. TSgt Russell remained in his ivory tower that whole time, calling out callsigns and directing precision runs with his laser designator.

"Stand by, Vapor. Airburst, fifty feet, all three racks, marking coordinates with laser, thank you."

"Frost, designating city block for two-thousand pounder, try not to miss, thank you."

"Talon, I read you loud and clear. You'll want to bank and release on this one; don't want you in the Navy's bombardment corridor, thank you."

The noise was something else. Even with ear pro in and inside the airport terminal, my chest shook with the constant bombardment. Every ten seconds, another rack of six bombs detonated airburst, ripping the massed ranks of zombies apart with lethal shrapnel. In the distance, two-thousand-pound GBU-32s vanished into the windows of buildings and blasted entire structures to rubble in columns of black smoke. The debris fouled the zombies' advance, forcing them to mass up, and Russell directed airburst sorties against these targets.

In the distance, bigger explosives detonated, shaking the ground beneath us. MOABs and fuel-air bombs shattered what felt like the entirety of the 22202 ZIP code. Bodies were thrown so far, we kept seeing corpses chucked into the river from the explosions. Some even hit the roof of the airport.

The Air Force left the bridges standing, though. They wanted the millions of Zs to keep running right into that kill zone. And the Zulus obliged.

Thousands were being slaughtered every minute. The smell was ungodly; a mix of acrid explosive, charred metal and concrete, and rotten, liquefied flesh. We couldn't see a thing anymore for all the smoke and dust choking the air.

"Want one on the bridge?"

"Negative, let 'em into the kill zone, Specter. Appreciate the offer, thank you."

"You got it. Happy trails."

Freaking Air Force.

Every now and then, one or two Zulus made it through the hell outside into the terminal. We called them out and dropped them as they appeared. Furry used Gunny's M9 now, his SAW no doubt a twisted hunk of gunmetal somewhere out there.

But the zombies kept coming.

They were concentrated now. Cavanaugh's tactic had worked, and now the combined dead of Washington D.C., Arlington and Quantico surged towards us like a heaving sea of rotten meat. Wave after wave of zombies rushed at us, uncaring of the broken ground, the shrieking bombs, the fighter-bombers roaring overhead. They didn't care about the A-10s strafing the streets with Avenger 30mm cannons; thirty-nine hundred rounds a freaking minute just shredding concrete and flesh. They didn't care about their buddies getting literally aerosolized by the weapons of the US military.

The Zs just kept coming.

A regular army would have shattered from the losses. Just one strafing run would have been enough to break any normal advance and make infantry dig in for protection. They didn't care. They ran for us, crawled, dragged themselves. We picked off dozens of ruined "survivors", incapable of dying from the shock of their annihilated bodies, as they dragged themselves into the airport. To conserve ammo, we used hammers, fireaxes, and cinderblocks.

Of course, Furry tried one time to use his boot, but he hit the thing at a glancing blow and wound up hitting the deck next to it. Dom had to step over and stab the Z in the brain before it could pull Furry's frantically kicking leg into its mouth.

That whole time, Dakota's broadcast blasted its siren call out into the city, calling every undead man, woman and child to their second death. The planes dropped their bombs, the Navy blasted the city, and the Marines shot, clubbed and stabbed everything else that made it close.

The plan was working. It was *working*.

At least, until it didn't.

Not when the bad guys showed up.

Chapter 24 - CLEAN UP

I think we were two hours into the bombing when it happened. The world shook every time a Raptor dropped its load. The glass in the back of the terminal had long since shattered completely, unable to handle that many explosions so close. It was nice to have the circulation; the stench of evaporated zombie was becoming something akin to smog. Fortunately, the sea breeze seemed to be working at clearing it out.

I saw movement crawling through the doorway, and I sighed.

"Roach," I said, using Furry's newly-coined term for a Z that had survived the apocalypse outside. "I got it."

It was half a roach. This Z had one arm and no legs, dragging itself inside the airport through the power of its hate. Its fingernails were ripped and bloody, and I almost had to admire it. It had probably taken a ton of work to get in here.

"Sorry, buddy," I said, lifting the axe. "Sucks to be you."

One chop later, I wrenched the axe head out of its rotten skull and turned away. These things gave off a serious smell in close-quarters combat, like sewage left to fester too long.

Then I heard Russell break from his usual instructions to the pilots over the net. I had mostly tuned his Texas drawl out by this point.

"Hey, Command, I got an unidentified bogey in my airspace, you know anything about that?"

"Uh, negative, Ghostrider, just our squadrons."

After a second, Russell said, *"Command, it looks like an AH-64 Longbow. Why's the Army got an Apache in our flight corridor?"*

"Unknown, trying to raise it now."

"Command, it's turning and heading for our location. Did you send us visitors?"

"Negative, your evac is still en route."

"10-4, will try to raise them. Unidentified chopper, you are in congested air space. Highly suggest you break off, friend."

"Friend" was TSgt Jon Russell's last word.

I didn't hear the M230 chain gun spin up; that would have been impossible over the bomb drops. But I heard the volley of 30mm high explosive incendiary rounds shrieking through the air. To this day, I think I heard Dakota scream just before the Apache dropped two seconds of sustained fire into the top of the air traffic control tower.

My head snapped up to a skylight to see the tower shedding metal like scales. Flames, explosions and smoke filled the interior, then the pair of Hydra rockets struck, burrowing into the tower's guts and blowing it apart in a ball of fire and shrapnel. Debris showered down onto the roof, and I screamed, "Marines, take cover!"

On my radio, I heard him. *"Hat's off to you, meat. You survived a real storm out there."*

It was Thompson.

In my mind, I still saw SSgt Harrison crawling over the helipad of Detrick, one hand to his gut wound, face clenched in pain as the Blackwater thug stepped up and capped him in the back of the head.

"Surprised you're still alive after everything the doc has sent after you. Now she sends me, along with her regards."

We were spread across the terminal, looking for the survivor scraps. Sanchez and Ferreira were at the north end, and I twisted toward them, just in time to see the Apache swing behind the terminal, level with the completely open back end of the airport.

"Sanchez, Ferreira, hit the deck!" I roared, but it was too late. The gunship slid sideways, level with the terminal, and strafed the entire north end. The two Marines disappeared in a hail of 30mm incendiary, Furry trying to throw his body across Sanchez in a vain attempt to protect her before the rounds tore through both of them.

"Two more down, Slaughter. How many you got left?"

"Sergeant!" Gunny roared. "Fall back!"

The black was taking my vision again. *We had been winning. We'd actually been* winning.

On other channels, I heard confused pilots. *"Designator signal's lost, please advise. Do I drop, what do I do?"*

I roared into the mic, "Taking fire from hostile gunship. Apache helicopter, Marines down! Take it out!"

Gunny grabbed the radio from me. "This is Gunnery Sergeant James Hudson. The airport is lost, I repeat, the airport is lost. Commence grid bombardment on our location."

"Negative on that, Marine, we do not have designator for precision bombing and you are not clear."

"We're dead anyway!" Gunny yelled. "Do it now!"

A second, then *"Acknowledged. Commencing grid bombardment."*

The Apache hovered for a second, then turned toward us, its profile menacing.

"Hey, jarhead. Dance."

Rockets sprouted from the pods on its sides, and I hurled myself as far as I could. The rockets landed about thirty yards short, but the blasts still ragdolled me across the terminal.

I hit the ground and rolled, trying to bleed off the momentum. I screamed as shards of glass from the shattered windows knifed into the muscles of my back.

I surged to my feet, breathing hard, lurching toward the other end of the terminal. I saw Dominguez, holding open the stairwell door and shouting. I couldn't hear anything over the ringing in my ears.

No, that wasn't right. For some reason, I could still hear Thompson, growling through my earpiece.

"You embarrassed me, jarhead, embarrassed me professionally, and I happen to take that a little personal. The doc told me not to come back til you were zombie kibble."

I kept hopping toward Dominguez, but I heard the chopper shift over behind me. The bastard was holding his fire, making me sweat.

"So long, meat. This shouldn't hurt... much."

I heard the gun spin up. I threw myself towards Dominguez, knowing I was way too far away to make it.

I hit the ground and rolled to see my death, hovering just outside the airport. I could see Thompson through the canopy, grinning like a sadist over the stick. He wanted me to see him. He wanted eye contact.

So as locked on me as he was, he didn't see Gunnery Sergeant James Hudson.

Gunny rose to his feet out of the burning rubble like an angel in MARPAT. In one hand, he held his Benelli M1014 shotgun. In the other, an M67 fragmentation grenade, pin removed, cooking in his hand.

I saw Gunny's lips move clearly, though I couldn't hear him over the bombs, the chain gun, the ringing in my ears. I did hear him over the radio, though, clear as day.

"This, on the other hand, is going to hurt a lot. Have fun burning in Hell, you disgusting stain."

He blasted the shotgun one-handed at the cockpit, five rapid-fire blasts. Thompson flinched back as sparks jumped off of the fuselage, and his attention was drawn from me for just long enough.

Gunny side-armed the grenade at the chopper, yelling, "Run, Sergeant!"

I obeyed, running as fast as I could limp toward Dominguez while keeping an eye on the chopper. Distracted by the shotgun blasts, Thompson didn't even see the explosive til it banged on his canopy. The thug's eyes widened, and instinctively he jerked the stick hard as the grenade exploded.

Flames wreathed the canopy as shrapnel struck sparks from the metal. That alone was unlikely to down the gunship; it was armored against RPGs and other small explosives.

But Thompson panicked. He was jerking the stick, trying to pull away from the explosion, and his rotors chopped into the ceiling of the airport. The blades made it through two chops, then stuck fast. Instantly, the tail swept around as the helicopter spun crazily and slammed into the floor of the airport.

"Gunny!" I roared.

The last I saw of him, Gunny Hudson stood tall in its path, his shotgun at his hip, fearless in the face of Death. Then the Apache finally exploded, wrapping wings of flame around him and taking him from sight. The detonation blasted me closer to Dominguez, who grabbed me and started hauling me away.

As glass sliced into my hands, as my back burned from the intense heat, I screamed Hudson's name over and over.

****

Dom dragged me into the metal stairwell and locked the heavy door. He pulled a first aid kit out of my pack, supplemented by his IFAK, and had my burns and wounds cleaned and bandaged in a snap.

And there we sat, processing our grief as the bombs kept exploding outside. Thompson's attack happened two hours in. The Air Force kept hitting our area for another three.

With Russell's designator gone, precision bombing was a joke. The Air Force continued to rain down bombs on the now-aimless hordes, but without that laser, plenty of them made it into the ruined airport. A crowd of them banged on the door and howled at us through the tiny window even now.

Dakota's signal was down, and the Zs were reverting to their original state, hunting targets of opportunity.

I didn't care.

I had lost every single member of my squad except one, because of man's petty games. We'd handled zombies just fine. It was the ones supposedly on our side that killed us.

Then I looked up and saw Dom. Streaks of tears lined his face. His dark eyes were older than I'd ever seen them, and I saw a young man struggling to hold it together.

I knew that look.

And I knew how Gunny Hudson would have taken care of

it.

I moved over to my Marine, put an arm around him and let him sob into my shoulder.

Epilogue

The Navy sent a chopper of Marines to dig us out. Turns out, most of the airport had collapsed in on itself. The pilots did their best to avoid blowing us apart, which I was very thankful for and made sure to do so in person later.

A full squad of Marines roped onto the shattered runway, blasted through the crowd at our door, and wrenched the thing open. They pulled us out and basically carried us to the chopper.

Two minutes later, we were airborne, heading to Kent Island.

When we got there, Dom and I stared.

Man, the bridge was filled, *filled*, with civilians. American families waited in lines to board boats that would take them to the fleet tender that would evac them all out.

"How many is that?" I rasped, my throat savaged from the smoke inhalation and shouting.

The squad leader who'd grabbed us, somebody named SSgt Mendoza, glanced at me. "Last count? A few thousand, probably more. I don't know what it is now; they're trying to call in more ships to handle them."

Dominguez met my eyes, and we took a deep breath. I leaned over and said in Dom's ear, "This. This is what Alpha died for."

"Rah, Sergeant," Dom answered, sniffling and looking up.

When we touched down, Sgt Major Hawke was there to meet us, along with an honor guard of Marines. When we staggered off the chopper, the cheering started.

All around us, Marines and servicemen clapped and shouted as the chopper blades spun down. "Oorah!" they roared. "Alpha leading the way!"

I limped up to Sgt Major, leaning on Dominguez. "Good afternoon, Sergeant Major."

His eyes ran up and down me, taking in the wounds, the

blood, the grit. He saw Dom, and he saw who was not there. I saw deep pain in his eyes, and a sympathy no civilian would ever be able to offer.

"Good afternoon, Sergeant Slaughter," he said, his voice tight.

"Slaughter Squad!" the Marines shouted. "Slaughter Squad!"

"What is this?" I asked, gesturing at the celebration.

Sgt Major glanced at me. "It's not just for you, Sergeant. This is the first victory we've had against the biters. United States Marines led the way, devil dog, and you led those Marines. Now we know we can fight them, and everywhere there's a radio, they're hearing about the evacuation of Washington D.C. and the last stand of Slaughter Squad."

He looked me over. "Looks like you need a doc and some chow, Marine."

I hesitated. It didn't feel… right.

"Need to put in awards," I said awkwardly.

Sgt Major stilled. This wasn't the right way to do it. There was paperwork to be done, but this needed to be said.

But Hawke did it anyway.

"All right," he said. He pulled a notepad out of his breast pocket, along with a pen. "Names."

And I told him. LCPLs Dakota, Marshal, Sanchez, Turnboe and Ferreira. CPL Sloane. CPL Garrett. LCPLs Park and Solomon. SSgt Harrison. TSgt Russell of the United States Air Force. The Marines of Alpha Squad, 3rd Fireteam: Gutierrez, Martinez, Turner and Stevens.

Gunnery Sergeant James Hudson.

When I stopped, Sgt Major flipped his notebook closed and replaced it in his pocket. "Done, Sergeant. Go take care of yourselves. Now."

I glanced back at Dominguez, who slowly shook his head.

I looked back to Hawke. "Not sure that's in the cards for us, Sergeant Major. What can we do around here?"

He chewed on that for a moment, looking from me to

Dominguez. "You wanna work? Fine. Colonel Santiago and Captain Hayden have been discussing amphibious assault teams to clear out coastal communities and evac trapped civilians. Go find him and lead that."

I looked at Dom, who nodded. A light had reentered his eyes.

"What do you think, Marine?" I asked. "No one lives forever."

Dominguez held up a hand, and I clapped it in mine.

"Semper die," he said.

Oorah.TO BE CONTINUED ...

ALSO BY JONATHAN SHUERGER

The Shades of Black Series
In Darkness Cast
Afterlight
Knightfall (coming soon)

Shades of Black Origins
Son of Anak
Blood of Anak
Ashes
The Raising of Ermog Grei
Desolate
Einherjar

The Exorcism Series
The Exorcism of Frosty the Snowman
The Exorcism of Tiny Tim (coming soon)

IST Marines
Semper Die

ABOUT THE AUTHOR

Jonathan Shuerger is an award-winning author and Marine Corps veteran. He has independently published the *Shades of Black* series and the *Exorcism of Frosty the Snowman,* but when J.F. Holmes asked him to write a novel set in the world of *IST* from the viewpoint of U.S. Marines, he couldn't turn it down.

Jonathan served as a USMC Arabic cryptologic linguist with 1st Radio Battalion in Camp Pendleton, eventually becoming senior linguist on the watchfloor. He is also a 3rd-degree black sash in Temple Chinese Boxing, dad of (currently) 5 little girls, and husband to a very loving, very patient wife.

Learn more about him at **https://jonathanshuerger.com** and join his newsletter to learn about his upcoming releases.

ACKNOWLEDGEMENTS

Thanks to the Gun Crew at Cannon Publishing for pitching in their expertise when asked what 5.56 rounds would do to rotting corpses based on how many days it had been dead, etc. Great beta reading, helpful feedback. It's a great group of men and women to write with.

Thanks to J.F. Holmes for letting me dirty up his pretty *IST-1* universe with my Marines.

Thanks to Bill Erwin for his edits. Any mistakes you see are his. ☺

Thanks to my Marines from 1st Radio Bn, who pitched in their ideas and jokes to form Alpha Squad. You guys are the only thing I miss about the watchfloor, and pretty much all I remember.

Thanks to my wife Amanda for her patience with her insane husband and his devil dogness. You're an angel, babe.

Finally, and ultimately, thanks be to God for His love for Marines.

More Books from Cannon Publishing

The Fae Wars

An ancient enemy invades Earth, returning to claim their home world. The men and women of the US Military find themselves matching technology against magic as cities burn and armies clash.

Onslaught
The Fall
Futures Past
Tales from the Occupation: A Fae Wars Anthology
Insurgent
Ghost
Northwest Front

In July of 2016 a plague swept the world, and the civilization collapsed and fell. For a lone National Guard sergeant, a veteran of the wars overseas who had settled down to a new life, the nightmare began on a hot summer evening at the barricades. Orders and chaos, gunfire and being overrun, his unit dwindles away in the face of the infected.

Months later, living in the ruins, the thud of helicopter rotors followed by a crash and the rescue of a downed pilot leads Sergeant First Class Nick Agostine back into the arms of the US military. From his experience comes the idea of teams, military and civilians experienced in dealing with the undead and barbarism of the wilds. The first Irregular Scout Team leads the way for Task Force Liberty to advance down the Mohawk Valley in Upstate NY, making contact with survivors and clearing out the infected with stealth and firepower.

Volume 1
Volume 2
Volume 3: Civil War
Volume 4: Bad Company

The Line

When the world descends into chaos and anarchy with an unbelievably swift plague, turning victims into ravenous maniacs, the soldiers of America's storied 1st Infantry are asked to hold the line. From the brutal streets of urban combat to the bloodied, desperate defense on the plains of Kansas, they fight a war against an unrelenting enemy who used to be their fellow citizens.

As civilization falls, can they hold the line?

The Thin Dead Line
Dead Storm Rising
The Big Dead One

Fallen Empire

What's a soldier to do when the war is over? When he's only known conflict his whole life? Since time immemorial the solution has been to find another war, this time for pay. Whoever has the credits and wins the high bid gets the experienced fighter. Sometimes, though, the credits aren't enough to cover the price.

Empires rise, but Empires also fall. The Terran Union has spent five centuries under the control of the alien Grausians, like a barbarian tribe under the thumb of Rome. Now, after almost two decades of civil war and succession struggles, the formerly subject races have settled back in their ancient territories to lick their wounds and re-arm, leaving hundreds of settled planets to exist in a political vacuum.

Into that space steps the free companies, mercenary units that fight for gold, honor, power and glory. Veterans who can't get the wars out of their souls, new recruits looking for adventure, corporations with their own agenda.

Join us in a 27th Century that echoes history.

The Irish Brigade
Overrun
Silent Violence

The Professor has problems, and not just what decades of soldiering did to his back and his knees. His boss just died, leaving him as CEO of the extremely discreet intelligence contractor Athenaeum, Incorporated. His old buddy the Operations Director is a highly skilled Army Ranger veteran but his finance chief is slightly unhinged and spends her money on highly inappropriate work outfits. The surviving old men on the Board of Directors are stuck in the 1970s. Running Athenaeum out of an old Cold War bunker and keeping their roster of experts together is expensive, but the government contracts are drying up or going to bigger, flashier corporate players.

Door Number Three
Doubling Down

Offworld

When nuclear war erupts on Earth, the American colony in the Alpha Centauri system is left stranded. As the new day dawns, a furious attack by the native inhabitants threatens to overwhelm the colony's defenses. It's left to the thin red line of the US Army's 9th Regiment to stem the tide and ensure humanity's survival in this harsh new world.

From two time Dragon Finalist and author of the best selling series "Irregular Scout Team One" and "Invasion" comes a new tale that tells of the struggle for survival on a brutal planet.

Offworld: Ragnarok
Offworld: Expeditions

Valkyrie

Humanity engages in a desperate struggle with an alien species for this side of the Orion Arm. Space ships die in instantaneous bursts of light and turn into vapor, but on the ground Marines scream and lie wounded in the mud and blood, praying for the Valkyries to come save them.

They aren't wishing for death and a Nordic goddess to take them to Valhalla, the wounded are praying for the men and women of the '348th Field Hospital MEDEVAC to dive through fire and hell to come save them. Because they know that ...

Valkyries never die!

Valkyrie
Valkyrie: Rebellion
Valkyrie: Attrition

High Caliber Awards

The Cannon High Caliber Awards are an annual contest for new writers. In it we ask them to submit a novella length story of Science Fiction, Military or Fantasy genre to challenge their skills.

2024
2025

The Wishkiller Saga

While on patrol Captain Aethal Paaling discovers evidence that an ancient terror has reached the rich soil of his home: the Lotus, a prolific growth whose addictive leaves devour their victims from within turning their hosts into horrible, terrifyingly violent mockeries of humanity. Created at the dawn of history by the twisted power of a godly relic called the Well, the return of the Lotus may be a harbinger of even more horrors to come.

Carrying the fatal news to the capital, Aethal discovers that even in the face of death itself, the Lords Paramount of Verlaen will fight to keep their secrets and their power. With only the guidance of his legendary Greater Rifle and the aid of the Pheonix Lancers, the soldier must find his way through the halls of a forgotten holy order and into deep dens of crime seeking answers.

He must find the truth as quickly as he can, because the Lotus may have already taken root among those he loves... and fighting it may cost him everything, including his soul.

Hexen

When nine out of ten people in the world have died in a brutal plague, what do those who remain do to pick up the pieces? Does the creed, "Duty, Honor, Country" have a place any more if there's no country left?

On his way across the devastated remains of Texas, Marine Corps veteran and survivor Eric Marten rescues a young woman from a vicious attack by men who have turned into savages. As Dani slowly learns to trust him, they try to stay alive in the deathlands that America has become, using all their wits to survive a post-apocalyptic nightmare.

90% Death Rate: A Post Apocalyptic Thriller
Angel of Death: A Post Apocalyptic Thriller
The Bloody Princess: A Post Apocalyptic Thriller

Hell Train

**A single train carries what might be the last vestige of
civilization through a hellish nightmare.**
A few hundred alive out of millions, lights going out all
across what was once America as the possessed arose from
the dead and murdered the living. A few hundred survivors
travel across the country in an armored train, seeking some
place to shelter in a fallen world. All that remains is a
dystopian nightmare marked by rains of blood, impossible
horrors, and portals to Hell opening in the skies.

US Army Captain Jack Zamora is responsible for their safety,
a self-imposed burden that wears on him every day. Fighting
off undead, protecting the survivors, keeping the train
running and supplied as his team desperately plans their next
moves. Starvation and disease threaten. but it gets worse,
because the ancient gods have sent their emissaries, horrific
beings of myth and legend that walk the Earth. Things that
can drain a man's very life essence or even that of an entire
city.

Hell Train: All Aboard

The Path

**Sometimes a hero isn't what you expect, and the one you
need comes from the castaways of society.**

Nearly broken and at the end of his rope, former decorated
scout pilot and prisoner of war, Red has finally accepted the
inevitable. He and his kin have no future in the Human
Confederation of Worlds, being gene mods and barely human
themselves. With the help of his friend he flees Terra for
adventure and fortune out in the reaches of the galaxy. Along
the way he's dragged back into conflict that calls on all his
piloting skills and he learns the deeper meaning of Kin, as his
crew becomes his family.

Path to Freedom: The Path, Book One

Invasion

More than a decade after the Confederated Earth Forces were defeated, their commanding general, a boyhood protegee, lives in exile and disgrace. His life on an isolated farm is forever changed when two strangers show up at his homestead, and the war comes crashing back down on him. The problem though, remains the same. How do you fight an enemy that is technologically superior and holds the high ground?

Invasion: Resistance
Invasion: Day of Battle
Invasion: Total War

The military experience is timeless, and echoes down from our past and into our future. Along the way, not everything is as it seems. Thirteen stories from established and new writers in the field of Military Science Fiction and Military Fantasy bring you tales of the terrors of combat and the even greater fear of the unknown in Cannon Publishing's first Bi-Annual Military Anthology.

Fifteen classic Science Fiction stories from both masters of the craft and up and coming new writers!

A tyrannical United Nations pulls the strings of its colony worlds, ruling with an iron fist. Corporate interests take precedence, and brushfire rebellions smolder on the edges. One system, home to the only alien species yet discovered, with human allies throws off the yoke and calls itself Independence.

Feedback from the slight pressure of a hand closing sends a powerful mechanical arm smashing into an opponent. A neural link hurls blustering plasma fire from your suit's shoulder mounted cannon. Your reactor levels scream with overload as return fire smashes into your armor, and damage alarms wail while you hurl your twenty ton body sideways for cover.

You're a Mecha, a mechanical fighting machine with a human pilot. The guy that the infantry curse at in training and pray for in combat. The machine that the last hopes of your people ride on. The construct that strikes fear deep into alien hearts as they hear your turbines power up. The one able to pass through hell and come out the other side victorious, or die trying.

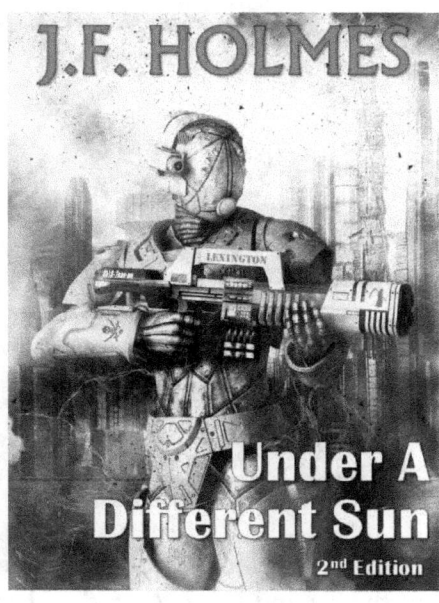

In the near future, massive empires rule the stars, and west of the Reach, they are battling for control of new systems. In the no-mans land between the front lines, Captain Nate Meric and the crew of the privateer Lexington fight for prize money, and loyalty to their ship and their friends. Beneath it all, though, runs a hidden dream. To see America restored, and take her rightful place among the stars.

Sea of Fire: Demonrise

Brian Corel, former slave, gladiator, ex-fiance to an Empress, exiled Captain of the Taland Royal Guard and now owner of the frigate *Widowmaker,* does the best he can to balance the lives of his crew with his own desire to live life as a free man.

Skirting the border between being a privateer and an outright pirate, Corel stumbles into a war with a religious cult intent on corrupting the kingdom of an old friend and has to set things right while grieving over his lost love. Along the way he signs a dragon into his crew and has to risk everything to rescue his brother from the grasp of a demon that has destroyed an entire continent.

Chosen by the Sword

There are some things a PhD doesn't prepare you for, like running two feet of steel through the guts of a flesh-eating monster straight out of a nightmare, while ducking razor sharp claws. Or having the sword critique your fighting style while you do it.

Dave Howard had a problem. Last week, he was out looking for a teaching job in the middle of a wrecked job market. This week he was neck deep in green blood and hellfire. Dragged into it by the very sword, his grandfathers' mysterious possessed blade, that was now walking him through hacking up a ghoul without getting his own head cut off. This wasn't exactly what he had gone to school for, and the University he had just taken a job with seemed to be anything BUT an academic institution. More like some kind of monster hunting bunch of weirdo nerds. Maybe his degree in Personality Psychology might be useful there, at least. The fighting though … as he dodged another swipe of claws and awkwardly tried to follow the instructions the sword was screaming at him, he shot back at it, "Hell, I'm Canadian! Swordplay isn't in my cultural DNA!"

Beyond the Wall: A Novel of Post-Roman Britain

The legions are but a memory, the glory of Rome only a shadow of crumbling ruins and broken walls.

A darkening tide of barbarism was washing across Britain's shores and the lights of civilization were slowly flickering out into darkness, only kept burning by the legendary Red Dragons cavalry unit. Led by their Tribune, Arthur, who serves no kingdom but goes where the fight is hardest and most crucial, they wage desperate battles to keep back the tide. The Red Dragons ride the length of Britannia to fight the invading Saxons, Scoti and Picts, wherever they show, from across the seas or down from the Highlands

At sixteen years old Peredur of Gwynedd has listened all his life to the stories of his father Pelinor fighting with Ambrosius Aurelianus. When word comes that his older brother has been slain in battle with the Saxons, his desire for revenge leads him to follow in his father's footsteps as a warrior, becoming a cavalryman with the Red Dragons.

Along the way he may either find himself a warrior and leader worthy of Arthur or be left lying forgotten in the dust of history.

Hell's Bells: War & Love Downrange

Two souls collide in the middle of a deadly war.

Sergeant Sylvie Lyons of Her Majesty's Royal Engineers wishes she'd listened to her grandda's advice and stayed away from the military. USMC Sergeant Hondo Cassidy wants nothing more in life than being a Marine and fighting.

Hondo and Sylvie find themselves thrown together when his artillerymen are assigned to provide security for her engineers deep in the desert of Afghanistan.. Amidst death, destruction, cultural misunderstanding and the inevitable that happens when you mix an all male unit of Marines with an engineer unit that is mostly female, Sylvie and Hondo find in each other a reason to live.

That is, if they can survive.